DEATH ON A QUIET DAY

MICHAEL INNES

"A singularly nippy chase which promises to drop of exhaustion a dozen times and each time meets so bracing a new menace that it leaps right up before it ever settles down."
— *New York Herald Tribune Book Review*

"Good humour abounds and the scenes of flight and pursuit are appropriately exciting."
— *Times* [London] *Literary Supplement*

"When Innes gets into one of his pure-action numbers, with the touch of fairy-tale unlikeliness which is another speciality, he's really wonderful."
— *San Francisco Chronicle*

ALSO AVAILABLE IN PERENNIAL LIBRARY
BY MICHAEL INNES:

DEATH ON A QUIET DAY

MICHAEL INNES

PERENNIAL LIBRARY

Harper & Row, Publishers

New York, Cambridge, Philadelphia, San Francisco
London, Mexico City, São Paulo, Sydney

DEATH ON A QUIET DAY. Copyright © 1957 by Michael Innes. All
rights reserved. Printed in the United States of America. No part of
this book may be used or reproduced in any manner whatsoever
without written permission except in the case of brief quotations
embodied in critical articles and reviews. For information address
Dodd, Mead & Company, 79 Madison Avenue, New York, N.Y.
10016.

First PERENNIAL LIBRARY edition published 1983.

Library of Congress Cataloging in Publication Data

Innes, Michael, 1906-
    Death on a quiet day.

    (Perennial library ; P 677)
    Reprint. Originally published: New York : Dodd,
Mead, 1957.
    I. Title. II. Series.
PR6037.T466D4 1983   823'.912   83-47586
ISBN 0-06-080677-X (pbk.)

83 84 85 86 87 10 9 8 7 6 5 4 3 2 1

CONTENTS

DEATH
ON A
QUIET DAY
MICHAEL INNES

i *DAVID HENCHMAN*

ONE DOESN'T EXPECT excitement on a reading-party. That's not the idea at all. A group of young men facing their final examinations within a year; a tutor, ambitious for his charges or merely amiable, prepared to spend part of his vacation in their company; comfortable quarters in some quiet country place, with hills that can be climbed or antiquities that can be inspected in the course of a long afternoon: these are the essentials. In the morning the young men pore over their texts, carefully underlining every third or fourth sentence, or pausing to copy whole paragraphs into bulging notebooks. Their tutor, who knows these to be virtually useless labours, is invisible in his room; he is writing a book which he knows to be virtually useless, too. In the evening the young men debate, argue, quarrel. At one moment they will be following with complete concentration some mild man with a flare for coherent discourse; at another they will be shouting insults at each other—having differing opinions on the limits of empiricism, or the principle of individuation, or the lesson of history being that there is no lesson of history. Their tutor, who regards this as the valuable part of the day's work, smokes a pipe, drinks burgundy (activities expected of him) and expertly sees to it that the hubbub goes on till

3

midnight. It can be quite good fun. But it is not exciting.

And, of course, it all has rather an old-world flavour. Reading-parties were much more the go in our grandfathers' time than now. The modern undergraduate is for the most part constrained in his vacations to go quietly home and batten on his parents—or he may get a job as a bus-conductor in Bournemouth or as a waiter in a holiday camp. The reading-party is a bit of a period piece. Villagers, while indifferent to American tourists, Scandinavian hitch-hikers, and whole bus-loads of their own urban compatriots, are inclined to stare at a reading-party, for they find the young men and their preceptor hard to make out. So one comes to feel that one ought to have whiskers, or an enormous moustache and protuberant Edwardian eyes, and be dressed in a Norfolk jacket and a high stiff collar. At least one supposes oneself —comfortably or uncomfortably—to be out of the world, and one doesn't remotely expect the world to come at one. Least of all does one expect it to put on a turn in which violent and mysterious events transact themselves against a background progressively revealed as likely to involve perturbation and crisis in high places.

But all this—or, to be accurate, rather more than all this—happened at Nymph Monachorum.

Who was she, and how did the monks behave with her? There are a good many place-names scattered around Dartmoor that lend themselves very nicely to flights of linguistic fancy about the nymph. Inwardleigh, Shebbear, Birch, Zeal, Laughter, Gerrydown, Cowsic, Childe's Tomb, Mole's Chamber, Little Mis Tor, Quintin's Man: these, and others not to be recorded, were built into the young lady's saga. Timothy Dumble, whose fresh-faced innocence would have warmed the heart of a Sunday-school teacher, was particularly resourceful at this endless game; it was he who found Chipshop, and who worked Cookworthy and Sheepwash into a single scandalous couplet. All this was fun, too, and old Pettifor, although he didn't himself compose limericks and the like, ajudicated upon their merits unperturbed. It was clearly a matter of pride with him never to bat an eyelid when his young men took this particular line. Presumably he had great faith in the salubrity of anything that indicated a lively mind.

This Rabelaisian vein was in any case only intermittent. If the young men hadn't been capable of a good deal of seriousness they wouldn't have been on Pettifor's reading-party at all. And Nymph Monachorum had presumably been chosen—by Pettifor himself—on more solid ground than that of its charming and enigmatic name. Pettifor was a bit of an archaeologist, and this was his part of the country; he was understood to have a brother in some sort of squirarchal condition not far off. Anyway, everyone agreed that the George was an admirable pub. If it was on the expensive side it yet provided notable value for money—and it did somehow happen that Pettifor's young men were never exactly bread-line boys. The other people who came—and they weren't a throng—came for the most part to fish; they had the appearance of being City men, Army men, Medical men—even of being rather distinguished men from time to time. But they were nearly all elderly men, and Pettifor's youths hadn't much to do with them. There was, it is true, a Colonel Farquharson, a sad man who hung around in a tongue-tied, sinister way and was too free with offers of drinks. And now for a couple of days there had been Dr. Faircloth, who was at once more conversible and more correct. He talked barrows and dolmens with Pettifor, and appeared to have a large hazy recollection of what Pettifor's young men

5

referred to as their "set books." Timothy Dumble declared that Dr. Faircloth was a retired clergyman of ample means, and somebody else made the triumphant discovery that he expected to be joined by a daughter in a day or two. There was a good deal of speculation about Miss Faircloth. No doubt if and when she turned up everybody would become entirely proper in their references to her. But until then she offered the same scope for imagination as did the Nymph.

Not that Miss Faircloth didn't have rivals. The George provided the academic party with a sort of common room in a large well-warmed loft; and, in intermittent attendance upon them there, several local girls and two Italian ones. These tripped about with hot buttered toast and jugs of draught cider at appropriate hours of the day; and in the evening they could be encountered in corridors dispensing hot water bottles. Pettifor's young men, whose knowledge of girls was roughly equivalent to their knowledge of outer space, flirted cautiously with these agreeable attendants, and discussed with inexhaustible sagacity the differences of national temperament they revealed.

A fortnight—the second fortnight in March—had passed in this pleasant but quite uneventful fashion. It was the first week of April that was another matter. And its drama —its violent and unaccountable drama—was preceded by a sort of curtain-raiser on All Fools' Day. This was little to do with what followed—at least not so far as any obvious chain of cause and effect was concerned. Possibly, however, it did significantly condition David Henchman's state of mind. David, that is to say, might not have acted quite as he did on some later occasions but for the rather absurd and uncomfortable episode in Timothy Dumble's car. The reader will be in a position to form his own opinion on this later.

It began with a discussion about Yanks and English. Leon Kryder, a Rhodes Scholar from Princeton, was more interested in this topic than in that of the Devon and Italian girls. He combined a large admiration for English institutions with a sober determination to exhibit those of his own country in a justly favourable light. Corresponding strengths, corresponding weaknesses: that was Leon's line. He was two or three years older than his companions, who regarded him with a wholesome awe masked beneath endless outrageous banter. To his patient and objective sociology they opposed extravagant statements based upon their devoted frequentation of American films in the cinemas of Oxford. On this particular evening Timothy had been moved to define the United States as the land of mixed-up kids. Leon Kryder had replied with an exposition of the greater burden of conformity to socially sanctioned behaviour-patterns that American adolescents have to bear. Although the individual has a great deal of freedom, it is only freedom to enjoy the same sort of freedom as everybody else of that age and that group.

Pettifor, puffing at his ritual pipe, said that this raised rather a perplexing philosophical point. There was a respectful silence, while his flock waited for him to elaborate. But he said no more—merely sinking deeper into his chair and staring abstractedly into the fire. Pettifor had fits when his pupils didn't seem to be in the forefront of his mind—a circumstance which always surprised them, for they owned all the healthy egotism of the young.

Ian Dancer said he saw nothing perplexing about the American conception of freedom. It simply deified the group. It was like Milton in *Paradise Lost,* declaring that freedom consisted in submission to his horrid old God.

What was wonderful about England, Leon pursued unperturbed, was the effortless self-confidence displayed by guys who stuck obstinately outside the bunch. For instance there was David Henchman. Look at him.

Everybody looked at David. And Timothy Dumble, shaking his untidy head, murmured "Pitiful . . . pitiful," as if there was really something that should arouse compassion in the sight.

David, Leon said, didn't participate in any activities on behalf of the college. ("Never seen on the old Campus," someone called out jocularly.) He didn't even attend club meetings. Yet nobody thought the worse of him. (Cries of "Don't we?" "David's a rotten outsider," "David's a harmless eccentric," "David's an unspeakable pariah.") But the vital point, Leon went on, was that David didn't think any the worse of himself. It just didn't occur to him that he was a rebel. If David disliked girls—which he wasn't known to do—he would take it for granted that he was entitled to dislike them as much as he liked. If David was exclusively interested in perfecting the technique of photographing mediaeval documents—an activity which he had never come within a mile of—he would suppose himself at liberty to do nothing else 365 days of the year. Well, that was fine. It came of generations and generations of settled social order, with every man knowing the privileges and duties of his station. And Leon Kryder didn't think it was a class affair; with a young English artisan, he supposed, it would be much the same. Yes, that was swell. But there was another side to the thing, all the same.

Everybody chuckled. There was always another side to the thing when Leon got talking. He was the most obstinately fair-minded man on earth. It was socially wholesome, he went on, that the community should take a pretty stiff toll of its non-conformists. On the one hand, it made the individual think twice before developing an unco-operative personality or sheerly egocentric aims. On the other hand it gave you a little *élite,* prepared to go on being rebels, even when the going was tough.

"You mean," Timothy demanded, "that David gets away with it too easily?"

Leon grinned. "I guess I quit being personal at this point, Timothy. But if America is a land of mixed-up kids, England is a cosily appointed paddock for stricken deer."

"But what about the mixed-up kids, anyway?" It was Ian Dancer, the youth who had cited *Paradise Lost,* that asked this. "What gets them going?"

"Being required to live beyond their income, I'd say."

"A sort of moral income?"

"Perhaps you could call it that. In the States we have this conformist slant, you see; and at the same time our ethos is competitive through and through. The result is a constant anxiety among our adolescents. Do they really belong to the group? Are they, as individuals, measuring up to it? They're always hankering to be put through something, and have tangible proof that they've made their grade. Hence the fraternities and initiations and what-have-you that you folk find so silly."

At this Pettifor roused himself from whatever he had fallen to brooding on. "There's something," he said, "in knowing what it's like to pass a test. In fact one should keep in training for it. Get flabby, and you may meet a crisis. And that's bad." He paused, and seemed aware that his pupils were looking at him in some perplexity, as if the context from which he was speaking wasn't at all clear to them. He sat up, conscientiously determined to achieve lucidity. "Of course initiations and ordeals are scarcely an American discovery. The authentic American discoveries are very few—although as it happens great importance must be attached to them." He paused again, and everybody felt on familiar ground. Pettifor would leave this little conundrum for anyone to chew on who cared to, and go on with his main proposition.

"Aren't initiations pretty primitive?" somebody asked vaguely.

Pettifor nodded. "No doubt. But the notion of passing into manhood by enduring a bad half-hour is very general. You get it outside primitive societies just as much as within them. Only it's not always half-an-hour. You should put in a little time, my dear Leon, investigating some of our public schools." And Pettifor looked round his flock with the slightly wolfish expression one could occasionally detect on his lean features.

"Ian, don't you agree?"

"My public school was a regular old Belsen, of course." Ian Dancer spoke with nonchalant pride. "But nothing to my prepper. And we weren't passing into manhood then."

"You were passing out of the nursery. It's another stage at which a brisk injection of confidence is needed."

"It was brisk, all right. But injection isn't technically quite the right word. David remembers. He was at the same place."

David nodded. "Yes—but I don't recall that we positively competed over what we could take. That seems to me utterly idiotic. Just think of the waste of nervous energy Leon endured before he escaped to civilisation for a while. There he was, with his natural aptitude for symbolic logic, or whatever it is. And he had to worry himself half round the bend wondering whether he was as tough as some half-wit in the same rooming-house. A rooming-house, incidentally, is what college-boys live in over there. And our Leon was just another neurotic college-boy."

10

"If you're not the most insolent crowd!" Leon, who was controlling an enormous flagon of cider, passed round the circle, liberally dispensing it. "And I don't remember all that waste of nervous energy. I husbanded it, rather. I knew what I'd need over here. The sweetest of tempers, and what's called a buoyant nervous tone." He paused before Pettifor. "How do I rate there, sir?"

"Very creditably, Leon. Alpha-minus-query-minus. And they are certainly a tiresome crowd." Pettifor swept the rest of his charges with an appraising glance. Whatever his odd preoccupation tonight, he'd been continuing to follow the talk with some part of his mind. "Still," he said, "they really do seek knowledge of your astounding country. They're hydropic for that, you might say, as well as for this endless cider. Tell them . . . let's see. Yes—tell them about playing chicken."

2 "But I've seen that! I've seen it on the flicks." Timothy Dumble announced this triumphantly. "It's precisely this business of proving to yourself that you're as tough as the other chaps."

"Is it done with a revolver?" someone asked. "A revolver with one of the six chambers loaded?"

"No. That's Russian roulette. Chicken is done with cars. You line up a lot of cars facing a sheer drop over a cliff. Then you all drive for the edge, hell-for-leather. The chap who jumps out first is the chicken. It's very simple."

There was a moment's silence, and then David spoke. "What about the cars?"

"Americans have no end of cars—isn't that so, Leon?"

"Sure. They just can't pile them over the cliffs fast enough, Timothy."

"Although I suppose chicken can be played only by the fairly substantial classes. Have you ever played it, Leon?"

"Not that kind, I guess. But there are others, in which you hazard a higher ratio of lives per automobile. What you might call over here utility chicken. And you don't need a cliff. A perfectly ordinary road will do."

"That sounds more our style." Ian Dancer's dark eyes

12

glinted above his pewter tankard as he threw off this. "Tell us more, Leon."

"You want a straight road, a bit of a slope, and handsome ditches on each side. You have four or five people aboard, all placed so that they can make a grab at the wheel. Off you go, with somebody steering only until you've got up speed. After that, the first man who touches the wheel is the chicken."

David shook his head. "Not nearly so good as the cliff," he said. "Lacks drama, while continuing to promise mess."

Ian put down his tankard. "You mean you wouldn't care for it?"

"Of course I wouldn't care for it." David spoke a shade shortly.

Timothy nodded. "Quite right," he said. "Chicken, if indulged in at all, should plainly be sumptuously dressed. Austerity chicken would be a bloody flop. Let's go to bed."

Old Pettifor was already on his feet. His business being with young men, singly and in groups, it is conceivable he had scented something he didn't care for. Certainly he was uneasy. "To bed, to bed, to bed; there's knocking at the gate," he murmured. "What's done cannot be undone; to bed, to bed, to bed."

They stood up and watched him from the room. It wasn't merely that he liked to mutter Shakespeare idly in his beard. He had reminded them of a brute fact.

But that night they played chicken, all the same.

Afterwards, David found he couldn't clearly tell why. But he supposed Ian to have been at the bottom of it. There had been two elder Dancers up at Oxford a few years before; and they were still legendary. Perhaps Ian had a wild streak by way of family endowment. Or perhaps he just felt obscurely compelled to measure up to his brothers—who by this time were probably staid and prosperous young bankers or brokers in bowler hats. There was no doubt that the chicken idea had power to get under the skin.

Certainly they weren't encouraged by Leon. The thing went through in the face of a sort of grim anger that was something quite new in him. He had declared instantly that he wouldn't play. Then he had gone off and had some carefully casual conversation with the landlord, who was working late cleaning up the bar. He came back and said briefly that he now knew a bit about doctors, district nurses, hospitals and ambulances. This did have a chilly effect, but it failed to stop the prank from going forward. Ian—this was David's guess—had taken it into his head to exploit a sort of smothered feud that existed oddly between the entirely good-natured Timothy and a man called Arthur Drury, who was entirely good-natured too. These two never jeered at each other, but stuck to an elderly politeness; probably neither could have explained in what the mutual irritation lay. Anyway, Ian had worked on it. David hadn't attended to the drift of the talk. He simply knew—out in the inn-yard and a clear moonlight —that the game of chicken was essentially a challenge between Timothy and this chap Drury, but that others were involved, including himself after all.

"You'll probably pile up your car," he said prosaically to Timothy. "And it won't be honest to fudge up a claim on your insurance company."

Timothy made no direct reply. He was the son of wealthy and indulgent parents—a fact to which he hated the slightest allusion. He flung open the doors of his big ancient tourer. "Muck in, chaps," he said. "We're going to find a hill."

14

Arthur Drury and Ian scrambled in beside him, and David found himself in the back with the two remaining members of Pettifor's reading-party. One of these, Tom Overend, he knew quite well; they had gone to tutorials together the term before. The other was a mere infant called Ogg—a freshman from another college, who was on the party only because he was Pettifor's nephew. Ogg hadn't yet done his National Service, but had grown a beard instead. He ought to be at school still, David thought, and a prominent member of the Field Club. He certainly oughtn't to be in this damned car.

"Drive on, chaps—drive on!" Ogg shouted this out so loud that there seemed a chance of his waking the whole pub. His voice was full of happiness. He was seeing life.

They drove through the village and out into open country. Finding what they wanted didn't prove easy. Most of the roads, narrow and winding, ran not between ditches but between high banks. An uncontrolled car trundling between these might be turned over; but more probably it would simply scrape and bump to an inglorious stop. When they caught a glimpse of anything else, it was of fields empty in the moonlight. Everything was alarmingly still. The only sound from outside the car was the chug-chug of Leon Kryder's motor-bike behind them. Leon was following, presumably, to do what he could. David, twisting round to have a look at him, was vaguely reminded of something sinister in a film. They swept round a bend and Leon vanished.

"Are we really going to be complete idiots?" Tom Overend asked this in David's ear. His voice was carefully not suggesting anything.

"It's quite crackers, if you ask me." David spoke casually too. "And this infant should be in its cot."

"What's that, old chap?" Ogg's face, flushed with

15

excitement, was turned to him.

David felt a sudden spurt of anger—he wasn't certain at what. "I said you ought to be in your cot," he repeated brutally. "Tucked up. Not out with the big, rough boys —rot them."

Ogg laughed wildly in his absurd beard. He was too keyed up to be offended. "Turn right!" he suddenly yelled. "Turn right, Timothy. There's a clear run downhill. I remember it."

The three men in front had been muttering together. It sounded like a quarrel. Perhaps Timothy and Arthur were at last blasting each other openly. But now Timothy swung the wheel and they were at once on a broader road that ran downhill before them into dimness. Ogg, blast him, had been right. David turned again and saw Leon swing after them. A Death-Rider in that fantasy of Cocteau's—that was it. Something between a speed cop and a Royal Automobile Club patrol—and waiting to convoy you to a nether world.

"You lot, behind—stand up and get so you can grab the wheel." Timothy continued to gaze straight ahead as he spoke, but David knew that he was now looking quite cool and placid. "I'm going to hold on till we get a bit of momentum, and then let go. After that, we wait for our preserver. Don't we, Mr. Drury?"

"Yes, Mr. Dumble. We do."

David didn't know whether to laugh at them or curse them. They might have been acting in some ridiculous college play, and trying to obey the producer's instruction to sound insolent. As for Ian, he had edged himself forward and sideways to allow the three behind to lean over the front seat, so that David caught a glimpse of his face. It was quite white and his mouth was moving oddly. And yet he was thoroughly dare-devil—a hard rider who was

16

due, David remembered, to ride in some Steeple-chase or Point to Point or other next day. You never knew what would take whom now. It occurred to David that he had no notion how he looked himself. But how he felt was another matter. It should be possible to inform himself of that. The answer, he found with some surprise, seemed to be pretty well covered by the word exasperated —or even by the extremely modest word cross. He glanced at Ogg. Ogg was exalted. The bearded brat might have been getting ready to gallop into the valley of death and save the guns—or whatever it is that people so gallop for in phoney poems. David wished he could get round behind Ogg and restore him to reality with a boot in the bottom. But that wasn't practicable. And now Tom Overend was talking again in his ear.

"There are ditches, all right, David my boy. Who's going to read out the rules?"

David said something obscene about the rules.

"Are you a chicken if you just jump?"

This time David didn't reply. He was wondering if it would be feasible for Tom and himself simply to pick up Ogg and pitch him overboard. He was particularly without a fancy, he found, for having to take the mutilated remains of Pettifor's nephew back to their nursery. But he had no time to pursue this possibility. The car was running gently downhill.

"This is it, chaps."

Timothy spoke unemotionally, and David suddenly judged his voice beautiful—an extravagant notion that had certainly never occurred to him before. And Timothy had taken his hands from the wheel.

So they were doing it—playing chicken. It was—in its small, silly way—incredible; it was like the knowledge that one's country is now at war. What's done cannot be

17

undone. Ogg had started to cheer.

The pace quickened. They were on the crown of the road and the car felt as if it would go like an arrow for ever. The headlights were on—without much effect in the full moonlight. But the beam just steadily skimmed the near-side ditch. David tried to glimpse the speedometer, but Ian's humped knees were in the way. They weren't yet hurtling, but the pace wasn't slow. There was no chance of a fiasco now—of their simply rolling gently into the ditch at the start. They were playing chicken; the game had begun; and there was nobody to blow a whistle.

But the wind whistled. It whistled in David's ear as he stood leaning over the front seat. That was an indication that they were getting up quite a lick. Ogg had quit cheering. Perhaps he had come out of it, and regained some rational notion of what they were booked for. . . . There was a terrific jolt. The car had gone over a pot-hole. That almost certainly meant . . .

Yes, it did. The shock had abruptly deflected their course, and they were heading straight for the ditch. Nobody *could* grab the wheel now, for there was nothing but a split second in question. This, as Timothy said, was it. The car would be the hell of a mess. And they would be very lucky if they themselves got off with broken bones . . .

Bump. When they seemed to be right off the road, and their near wheels in air, it had happened again. Incredibly, their course had shifted, and the clear road was once more in front of them—with an increasing gradient and a bend at the bottom. David heard Tom Overend gasp. It had been an absolutely fatal reprieve. For they were now moving really fast.

But David was no longer conscious of their speed. Suddenly he had become aware of nothing but his own hands. They felt enormous—like hands by Picasso in his period of elephantiasis. And they felt as heavy as if hewn out of granite.

It was the same with the others. David was visited by a quite clear intuitive knowledge of this. There were twelve hands in Timothy's car, and each weighed a hundred-weight. It had been entirely unimaginative not to know that that was how it would be. Or call it paralysis. Like the sort of dream in which terror clamps one's feet to earth, fuses one's tongue on the palate.

There was a lurch. Once more—but this time on a fine diagonal and with incredible momentum—they were headed for the ditch. David made a tremendous effort of will. His arms just wouldn't stir. He glanced sideways, and saw Ogg's face. And suddenly his arms were free, his hands were normal. He leant forward, clasped the wheel, and steered the car to the centre of the road. Timothy instantly and viciously applied the brakes. The car slowed down. The game of chicken was over.

Coasting down the hill on his motor-bike, Leon Kryder came to a halt beside them. His grimness was gone. "Well," he said, "now you know." He passed, and got no reply. "Scared dumb?" he asked cheerfully.

But he knew it wasn't exactly that. They were scared; it would be impossible to recover from honest terror that quick. But they were also awkwardly avoiding one another's glance; and Timothy had found a resource in getting out and feeling the brake-drums—muttering that they were lucky not to be on fire. What's done cannot be undone. They had played the damned game.

Arthur Drury was the first to speak. "Bloody nonsense," he said. He said it tentatively, as if fishing for the right note. Then, apparently satisfied, he conscientiously poured out all the bad language he knew—applying it impartially to Timothy's foul old car and all its moronic passengers. "Although David has a gleam," he ended up.

"Yes, David's a frightful ass." Tom Overend took it up quickly. "But—thank God—he can show an atom of sense at times."

"A fond, a foolish, but happily a trivial episode." This was Timothy's contribution as he climbed back into the car. "And now we go home."

"Yes, we go home," Ian said—and added: "Sorry about this, chaps."

Timothy glanced at him belligerently. "What d'you mean—sorry about this?"

"Started it, I'm afraid."

"Oh, shut up, for the love of mike." And Timothy tugged at the starter.

Only Ogg said nothing, and David's opinion of him went up. They drove off, and for a moment Leon stood by his bike, watching them. They had been damned lucky, he thought—and if the affair left them feeling awkward, that was all to the good. They wouldn't do it again. And they certainly had no future as mixed-up kids.

3 THE NEXT MORNING, David Henchman went off by himself. He'd have a quiet day. He quite often did this. It was what the others had in mind, he supposed, when they were shouting their cheerful nonsense the evening before—their nonsense about his being a pariah and a harmless eccentric. He had never himself thought twice about this mildly solitary habit of his—or certainly not to worry over it. For one thing, it *was* mild; he was never without his modicum of sociable occasions; and indeed if there wasn't some positively gregarious element smothered in him, he wouldn't presumably have come to Devon with this bunch of Pettifor's. Commonly, when he went off like this, it wasn't with any sense of making a break for a nervously necessary solitude. It was just a happening —as was getting back again and eating his dinner beside the next fellow.

But this morning it was rather different. He was glad there was still nobody in the dining-room when he finished his early breakfast; and he was annoyed when, getting outside, he came on Pettifor pottering round his old Land Rover. But Pettifor gave him only a cold and unseeing look. Probably he had got wind of the idiocy of the night before and wasn't too pleased. David didn't try to speak

21

to him. In fact, he damned Pettifor and Pettifor's lot roundly to himself as he pushed out of the pub.

He didn't however succeed in getting away with any cheery matutinal talk at all. As commonly in old places like the George, there was an archway one had to go under to reach the road. The room on top of this belonged to Dr. Faircloth—and there he was at an open window, smothering his face with lather. He might have been an advertisement for the stuff, so robustly and cheerfully did he confront the day. "Good morning!" he called out. "Off for a tramp?"

"I thought I'd go off somewhere." David felt ashamed of the lack of enthusiasm with which he made this response. If retired clergymen—supposing Faircloth really to be that—are able to greet life with glad cries while shaving, then it's only civil to do the smiling morning face business in reply. "Because it looks," David added, "as if it might be rather a decent day."

"I certainly hope so." Faircloth, thrusting his head further through the window, took a sniff and a gulp of day, rather as if testing it before allowing the waiter to pour out a glass all round. "Yes," he said. "It will be pretty good. How I wish I could come along."

"Then why don't you, sir?" David said this with exactly the casual cordiality required. Like all Pettifor's lot, David was a nice man with nice manners. And now, as he looked upward at Faircloth, he was interested to find that he could continue to smile engagingly while softly grinding his teeth. "There's a bus in ten minutes," he said. It wasn't perhaps too rash to allow a note of broader encouragement to these words. Faircloth, after all, couldn't have breakfasted. And he probably revelled in breakfast even more than he did in shaving-soap.

"Unfortunately I must just hang around. My daughter

turns up today, but I'm not sure when." Faircloth produced a safety-razor. "Where do you think of going? What about Knack Tor? It's a stiff climb, but there's a wonderful view."

David shook his head. At least he wasn't going to have his route planned for him. "I don't expect I'll do much. I've got some reading to do."

"Capital—capital." Faircloth stopped scraping at himself to nod vigorously at this. "A fine day, solitude, and the *Republic* in your pocket: it's not a bad definition of happiness."

David had to remember not to grind his teeth too loud. Retired clergymen—particularly if of ample means—are adept profaners of mysteries. "I must be off," he said, "or I'll miss that bus." He gave a wave—a nice man's wave— and then dived under the archway, scowling furiously.

The quiet village street was comforting, so that it was only half-heartedly that he damned Pettifor and Pettifor's lot once more as he made his way down it. As for Dr. Faircloth, he was a thoroughly decent chap. And here was the bus, that would take him straight away from all of them. He got into it and did a good five miles. Then he walked in the loneliest direction he could spot on his map. He lit his pipe. He swung the heavy, knobbly walking-stick that had been his grandfather's. He said scraps of verse aloud.

Well, that was all right. The knobbly stick, the pipe that was now so respectably ancient, his khaki shorts, his sky-blue wind-cheater, his well-worn Gunner's shoes: they were all extremely right and comforting. It was indeed a gorgeous day, with a light wind that you could get out of whenever you wanted to soak in warm spring sunshine. He found a sheltered corner by a stream and read for what he felt was hours and hours. Plato's subject was justice—

not an easy subject, it seemed. Once David looked up and said aloud—and rather to his own confusion—"The man can write." And once he filled another pipe. Then the sunshine became fitful for a time, and he decided to move on. He would get right up somewhere on the moor.

In the valley out of which he was presently climbing the stream was lined with heavily pollarded willows; they were thrusting up abundant withes of an astonishing red, like ginger-haired giants sprouting from earth, or explosions from a stick of accurately dropped bombs. At first he could hear tractors in the fields behind him and somewhere somebody was shooting. But presently there was nothing at all. He was on a narrow track the course of which was marked by posts carrying a single telephone wire; on every fourth or fifth post here would be a hawk, and as he approached, the bird would flap away, deceptively heavy like an owl, before rising and wheeling buoyantly over the empty moor. Presently he struck off across the turf. It was spongy in places, but he found it possible to tramp briskly more often than not. He had no goal in view—except that he vaguely felt himself to be looking for prehistoric hut circles.

David's imagination was much possessed at this time by the notion of unfathomable antiquities, by what Thomas Mann had called time-coulisses, by the sense that today's most immemorial legends had been equally immemorial legends long ago. So he climbed happily, his mind mooning around what he vaguely knew of the Early Iron Age. The sling—a new and deadly weapon—had advanced into Britain across this country. The hill-forts, with their multiple ramparts, were a memorial of that sort of warfare—outer defences of the coveted iron in the Forest of Dean. Then as now, battle had the same objectives—and they weren't romantic. Or almost the same. Iron then; oil or uranium today. And so with the weapons: now the guided missile; yesterday the smooth pebble or the baked clay bullet hurled from the leather loop. A sling would still be an engine to reckon with on bare ground like this. But he wondered if it had ever been any sort of weapon of precision, as the tale of David and Goliath would suggest. Or had it needed organised companies of slingers to be effective? He had an idea he'd read that in the La Tene culture things had been organised that way.

Mooning along like this, he hadn't been attending to the map, and presently he had a thoroughly satisfactory sense of having lost himself. Ahead of him, the moor rose to a succession of rock-crowned eminences. Two—a big and a little one—were close together; and he thought he'd now stop and identify them. It wasn't difficult. The little one was called the Loaf, and the big one was Knack Tor. It was Knack Tor that Faircloth had been burbling about, and that he himself had rather snootily turned down. Well, he'd have a go at it after all.

David strode on, peopling the next slope with lurking men in skins, in woad; imagining he heard the pebble or the flint sing suddenly past his ear. It was all nonsense—utterly remote from him, and yet quite easily to be conjured up in this way. Its charm lay in that. And he didn't, as he moved his ghostly warriors over the moor, cast himself for any hero's role. At least he wasn't childish enough for *that*—and anyway it was all too unformed and shadowy for drama. Now there was a lark singing above his head. Its song seemed to set a seal on the absolute silent surrounding him.

The effect of a great loneliness was remarkable; it was as if he had been in one of the uninhabited places of the earth. A quarter of a mile away two dark ponies were browsing, and nothing else moved. They might have been prehistoric creatures, innocent of human association. No new animal had been domesticated, David told himself inconsequently, since man first learned to leave any record of himself other than his bones. And there was no impress of humanity upon all this landscape except a false one: the piles of slabbed and tumbled rock on the summits of many of the tors. They looked like savage, like Cyclopian altars —so that one expected to see a thin curl of smoke going up from their flat tops. But it was merely the interior economy of the earth that had voided them and set them there; they possessed no meaning save what the fancy cared to lend them.

Knack Tor was now straight ahead. A tiny stream ran down from a spring on the shoulder linking it to the Loaf, and David followed this. The wind had sunk to nothing and he was still in bright sunshine, although to the south he could see a mist coming up from the sea. So entire was the silence around him that the small trickle of water at his feet seemed to hold all the elaboration of a symphony. It would have been impossible to chant aloud scraps of verse now—an act of presumption, of naked *hubris,* to be promptly visited with its due penalty by some indwelling spirit of the place. The height above sea level of Knack Tor was nothing tremendous—yet here in this bleakness and in its setting of lesser hills, one could easily endow it with all the magic of a great mountain.

David looked again at the tumble of stone at the top, and found himself pretending that here was something stiff and ultimate, a grim face of rock challenging the powers of climbers already exhausted by a long struggle from valleys almost infinitely far below. It was a silly fancy; one that would make Timothy and Ian and the rest think him an absolute sap. But perhaps they thought him that already? David paused in his tracks, frowning and aware of some elusive doubt about himself, deep in his own mind. Perhaps there *was* something queer in slipping away like this, without saying a word to anybody except the inescapable Faircloth. He turned and gazed back the way he had come, acknowledging an irrational sense that it would be cheerful to see one of Pettifor's lot—Timothy, Arthur, even the infant Ogg—trudging towards him. But the emptiness was complete; it seemed to extend right to the light mist that now formed the horizon.

He turned back and faced the Tor. A fine column of smoke was rising from the dark rude table of rock on the summit.

4   HE MUST HAVE been wool-gathering even beyond his common measure, David thought. For he had experienced for a moment, as he glimpsed that thin pillar of smoke on Knack Tor, the feeling they call *déjà-vu*—"this has happened before"—which usually comes to a mind off guard. Only it hadn't been, as it usually is, a sense of the repetition of something from his more or less immediate personal past. It was like coming again upon a sight familiar to him thousands of years ago, when smoke did go up from hills like these, no doubt—and upon some decidedly unpleasant occasions.

In other words—David told himself as he strode on—he had gone mildly dotty. It was what happened, one might suppose, if one went on imagining that one had a date with the Early Iron Age. In sober fact, what was happening up there was clearly a picnic; chaps preparing to boil a kettle or grill a chop. And this reminded him that he himself had set out without so much as a biscuit in his pocket. Perhaps he would pick up some sort of tea on the other side of the moor; and anyway there would be a good dinner when he got back to Nymph Monachorum.

It was rather consciously that David pursued these prosaic reflections; he wanted to be sure that it wasn't in the least a case of his imagination getting out of hand. And now he had probably better give the top of the Tor a miss. Whoever was there seemed to have scrambled to the very summit—which looked from here to be a slab of bare rock no bigger than a billiard-table, although it was probably a good deal larger. It seemed a funny place to cook. But there was no reason why he should butt in on the proceedings at what would necessarily be very close quarters. It was a nuisance; he had rather looked forward to the final climb; but he'd skirt Knack Tor and make for the Loaf instead.

This however was just what he didn't do. He continued on his former path. Precisely why, he didn't very clearly know. Perhaps he was recalling Faircloth's praise of the view. Or perhaps he was vindicating himself to himself as a reasonably sociable being. To look in on the picnic wasn't intrusive; in this lonely expanse it was merely companionable. He would climb up the rocks, exchange a word about the view with the people he found there, and then go on his way.

So David continued to climb. When his path grew steeper he was careful not to slacken his pace. The little column of smoke was an inconsiderable affair, but his first reaction to it had only yielded to an obscure and fanciful sense that it was important—even that it was ominous or threatening. At least it was a tiny scrap of the unknown. Perhaps it was a good principle never to turn aside from that.

The distance remaining to be covered was rather greater than he had thought. And now the smoke was fading. The kettle must have boiled, or the chops been done to a turn. It occurred to him that since he first saw the smoke there hadn't really been time for either of these operations. Perhaps the smoke hadn't represented cooking. Perhaps it had been a signal. David swung his stick and advanced with long strides. This was another notion out of his reading—rather earlier than that prompting him to fancies of sinister sacrifice on primitive altars. Reading, probably, about Red Indians. And it wasn't just a matter of beacons. There was a language of smoke. You manipulated a blanket over a smoky fire, and the result was a sort of morse-code done in puffs of the stuff. But there had been no puffs about the smoke from Knack Tor; just a single column going straight up in this still air. A signal like that would carry a long way. And it would need to, in this solitude. Apart from whoever was on top, there probably wasn't another human being within miles.

But this reflection had no sooner come to David than it was falsified by a single sharp report from somewhere ahead of him. Up here, too, there must be a chap out shooting. Goodness knew what, at this time of year. Perhaps there were hares. You could shoot a hare at any time. Except—he remembered Timothy telling him impressively —when there was an order to the contrary by the lord-lieutenant. Or perhaps that was in Ireland, where Timothy had grand relations. Yet Ireland could hardly run to lords-lieutenant nowadays . . .

That David Henchman's mind wandered in this way as he climbed shows that his feeling of there being something odd about the smoke on top of Knack Tor didn't go very deep. And certainly he wasn't prepared for what he found at the end of his final scramble. Not that scramble was quite the right word. In a small way, there was something like a real spot of climbing involved at the end—at any rate on the side from which he approached the summit. Nearly twenty feet of more or less perpendicular rock had to be negotiated, and although he found plenty of hand and toe hold he had to bring some concentration to the job. It didn't feel exactly alarming, but he wasn't an expert. He ended up rather ingloriously by crawling over the final verge on his tummy.

His first impression was that somebody else had completed this operation immediately before him. This of course was nonsense. He had been entirely alone. He was staring, all the same, at the soles of a pair of shoes. They were a man's shoes, with studs in them. David moved his head—it was an immediate and instinctive response to finding these things pretty well shoved in his face—and this gave him a view of the uppers. He was aware of pronouncing to himself the inconsequent verdict that these looked very good shoes. Then it struck him that they were the wrong way up, if this was really somebody doing a scramble like his own. The toes pointed skywards. David wriggled his thighs over the edge. He must have given his tummy a twist, he thought. It didn't feel nice inside.

A chap having a nap. That was it—nothing more. This great rock-structure on top of the Tor had the form of a shallow basin, and it was a perfect sun-trap on this mild spring day. So here was somebody asleep. David stood up. At his feet an elderly man was lying face-upwards on the rock. One arm was flung out oddly, the hand clasped over some small bright metal object. And the man had a hole in the middle of his forehead.

His tummy, David thought, had been ahead of his eye and his brain. Fortunately it didn't continue its demonstration. David took his eyes from the dead man—for he was certain he was that—and looked about him. In the very middle of this rocky saucer lay a little heap of ashes, with a tiny wisp of smoke still curling above them. That was what he had seen. He remembered that he had heard something, too. But what was it? He struggled with his memory and found that it had gone queer—which showed that you do get a bit of a shock when this sort of thing happens. What he had heard, of course, was the shot. And the glittering thing in the man's right hand was a revolver. He had killed himself. It had happened only a couple of minutes ago. Perhaps the man had seen David approaching, and that had hurried him up.

It came to David that he ought not, after all, to take it for granted that this motionless figure was dead. One heard of people surviving astonishingly the most frightful injuries to the brain. So what should he do? The body would still be warm. But there was the heart. He must feel the heart.

Fortunately he wasn't the infant Ogg. Once, in the Canal Zone, he had seen a couple of men meet instant death, and it had been his job to give reasonably collected orders. But there one had been gradually tuned up to the possibility of violence or misadventure. Whereas this . . .

He took hold of himself firmly and knelt down. The dead man seemed to have been in his late fifties. David remembered that sometimes you took to looking a bit younger again when you were dead. The forehead that had suffered such ghastly violation was broad and generous, and one would have taken the chap to be some sort of high-powered brainworker. Moreover, he seemed faintly familiar, so that for a moment David paused to gaze at his face. Perhaps he was the sort of middling-important person who gets his photograph in the papers from time to time. The hint of familiarity might be accounted for by that. Or perhaps what stirred at his recollection was not the man's features but just his deadness. It was, he repeated to himself, a sight he'd seen before.

And there was a job to do. But David hadn't put out his hand to the man's jacket before he was arrested by a sound behind him. He knew instantly what it was, for he had been making the same sound himself only seconds before. It was the scrape of a shoe on rock.

Somebody was coming up—but from the opposite side to that on which his own approach had lain. The sound was repeated a second later, not so loudly. It happened a third time—and David found himself very tense and still. There was a possibility that it wasn't somebody coming up. There was a possibility that it was somebody going down.

David took a deep breath, and finished the business on hand. It seemed the urgent thing. There was a cardigan to unbutton, and then he thought he had better get beneath the shirt as well. No, the heart wasn't beating; he was convinced of that. It was a grim bit of investigation, but he was confident he hadn't made a muck of it. Whoever he was, the chap had had it.

And now there was something else to find out about. David got to his feet again and ran to the farther lip of the basin. Here, he saw, there was a rather easier route up. There was nobody on it. But down on the moor, about thirty yards away, a man with a rucksack on his back was strolling past the summit of the Tor. At least that was how it looked.

As he had taken a deep breath to kneel by the dead man, so David now took another deep breath to shout. But he let it go unused. There was quite certainly no one else in sight. And he remembered that repeated scrape of a shoe on the rock. There was no rock down there—and, if there had been, the distance was too far for so small a sound to have carried. It sprang at David that the course the man with the rucksack was steering was a phoney course. The man had been up here. And he had climbed down again, put this respectable distance between himself and the summit, and then swung round so as to give himself the appearance of a casual passer-by.

Or—once again—that was how it *looked*. David realised that he had tumbled in upon something that was not merely a mess—like the mess that might have happened in Timothy's car the night before. He had tumbled in upon a mystery. Something had occurred of which the explanation might be very sinister indeed, and which set a perfectly plain suspicion before him from the start. Perhaps this wasn't a real suicide—although, if not, the revolver had certainly been disposed so as to suggest it was. Perhaps it was murder. Perhaps this man with the air of walking in comfortable ignorance past it all was a murderer. He had failed to spot David's approach to the Tor, and so had almost been detected in the very commission of his crime. But he had just managed to get away. And now he was putting on this innocent rural rambler's turn.

As he walked, he seemed absorbed in the view. But his interest didn't appear to be at all in the summit of Knack Tor. He was looking steadily in the other direction, where there was certainly a wonderful vista over the moor. In a few minutes he would just be a figure in the middle distance.

There is of course considerable comfort in seeing a person of possibly homicidal inclinations transport himself out of one's vicinity. David was rather taken by surprise at the strength of his awareness in himself of this simple human reaction. But it put extra vigour into the lungs with which he now did give a peremptory shout. "Hi!" he called—and immediately repeated: "Hi!"

The rambler gave no sign of having heard; he simply walked on. And now it was the turn not of David's tummy, but of his spine, to play a trick on him. A queer shiver ran down it, like a small electric shock. Unless the man below was deaf, it was quite impossible that he should have failed to hear. Possibly he was reckoning that although David had the guts to shout, he mightn't have the guts to come down and go after him. Well, he'd see. And for a start David shouted again. "Come back, please!"

At least he had hit on pretty significant words; they definitely announced his persuasion that the chap's stroll past was bogus. And this time there was a visible impact. The man stopped, looked round enquiringly at his own level for a moment, and finally—as if by a happy after-thought—let his glance travel deliberately upward until it rested on David. He raised a hand, as if to indicate that contact was established and further shouting needless. Then he advanced, deliberately and without haste, until he was almost directly beneath.

"Is anything wrong?" he asked. "Has there been an accident?"

5 DAVID FELT HIS confidence flicker. If the man had answered to his notion of a crook or a thug he'd have had a better idea how to handle him. But the man was like Pettifor —or if not like him then like some of the successful middle-aged men who came to Nymph Monachorum for the fishing. Authoritative and incisive, but at the same time benevolently disposed to the young. If he suggested anything particular it was perhaps a soldier—and one high enough up to be thoroughly affable in a clipped way. Not, you might say, the colonel. Rather a visiting brigadier.

This train of association was rather daunting. But David managed to say gravely: "Yes, something's badly wrong. I think you'd better come up here."

The stranger nodded. He might have been giving David instant credit for not being the sort of lad who fusses or flaps. Then he threw a rapidly appraising glance at the rocks. "It's not in the orders," he said, "but we needn't make any bones about that." And he slipped off his rucksack.

"Shall I come down a bit and give you a hand?" David wasn't at all sure why he said this. Perhaps he had noticed that the stranger's hair was iron-grey, and at once put him down as really old.

"That's very kind of you. But I've known rather worse bits. Gimmer Crag, for instance."

This was clearly ironical, and David said nothing. He watched the elderly stranger come up—it took him only a few seconds—and realised that his own performance on the other side of the summit had been a comically inexpert affair. It was going to be a bit of an effort, he saw, to keep hold of the fact that he himself must control the situation as it developed during the next few minutes.

And now the stranger was standing beside him, smelling of tweed and tobacco. His glance went instantly to the dead man. "Bad show?" he asked quietly.

"Very bad."

"Took a tumble, eh?" The stranger frowned. "But—dash it all—he ought to be at the bottom, not the top. You haven't hauled him up, boy?"

"Of course not." Despite the substantial horror of what he had been involved in, David found himself rather resenting this address. "And it hasn't anything to do with a fall. Just take a look."

The stranger walked over to the body and seemed about to kneel beside it. Then, as if he had suddenly read the unmistakable truth written on that forehead, he checked himself and turned rather slowly back to David. "My dear lad, it's not your . . . It's not a relation?"

"I don't know him. I never saw him before." David spoke abruptly. The man had been going to say "your father," and had checked himself. There had been quick kindness, controlled solicitude in his tone. It seemed almost impossible to believe ill of him. Everything counted in his favour, as far as the immediate stark issue was concerned—everything down to the way his moustache was trimmed.

David knew that judgment on these principles was

damned silly. It was even naïvely snobbish. One might as well judge the chap by his tweeds or his shoes. Incidentally, his shoes were just like the other fellow's—the dead man's. *And* his tweeds too. For what the point was worth, they were both from the same social bracket. They weren't exactly like Pettifor, after all. Pettifor was their unworldly brother, you might say. They themselves were the kind of men one used to listen to when one was in uniform and had to travel first class. They always had a boy who had just left Winchester to go into the regiment—meaning the Coldstreams—and who would eventually take over the family bank in Burma, if he shaped well.

David, as he thus rather imaginatively placed his companions, quick and dead, wasn't at all sure that he liked their tribe—if it *was* their tribe, and he wasn't simply romancing to himself as usual. Nevertheless he was habituated to paying it a young man's formal respect. And even if it was in some ways a particularly wicked class of society, he found it very hard to believe that gun-play on the summits of west-country hills was a common, or even conceivable, part of its drill. All this made it particularly difficult for him now to find and keep a line. Presently, and perfectly naturally, this chap—the living one—would be giving him orders. And that wouldn't do at all.

"You never saw him before?" The stranger, puzzled, was repeating David's last words.

"I do find something faintly familiar about him. But it's only some trick of memory, I think. In fact, I'm confident I never saw him before—and I never saw him alive, either."

"You mean, you didn't see him do it?"

"Do it, sir?"

There was a silence that seemed to David to last unbearably long. Into it, and into this high lonely cup of stone, a lark tumbled a glittering cascade of sound. David felt his heart pounding against his ribs. But he was satisfied with his last speech. He even felt his shoulders straighten oddly, as if some burden had been cut from them. And he smiled—so that the stranger was for the first time clearly startled. For some reason David was thinking tolerantly of Timothy and Ian and the others, and the game of chicken. What awful nonsense that had been!

"I mean, shoot himself, poor devil." The stranger contrived a note of patient explanation. "You can see the thing, can't you?"

"The pistol? Yes, I can see that. And I heard it, for that matter. You must have heard it, too."

The stranger shook his head. "I heard nothing until you started shouting. And then I took it to be a shepherd calling his dog."

David remembered that his shout had been decidedly unceremonious. It was, he supposed, just conceivable that it wouldn't have occurred to this rather commanding person that he was being bellowed at. "Don't you mean," David said quietly, "that you heard a shot, but simply took it to be somebody out having a pot at something?"

Again there was a little silence. It was heavy with the implication of David's words. The stranger, they asserted, might have thought up a more plausible line. But this didn't—immediately at least—draw any fire. The fellow just turned back to the body. "We'd better make sure," he said.

"You can be quite confident he's dead."

This time, the stranger gave David a glance of keen scrutiny. "I'm not quite sure," he said, "what's in your mind. But let an older man give you a word of advice. Just take it easy. An affair like this can be damned upsetting.

There's no discredit in feeling a bit rattled by it. Sit down. And I've got a drop of brandy, if you care for it. But barley-sugar's better—and I've got that too." He smiled. "Barley-sugar and a pocket compass are the first things to put in your pocket when you go walking. Of course, half-a-crown's useful, in case you feel like a bus at the end of the day."

David almost found himself sitting down. This easy magistral talk was undermining. But he glanced at the body, and stayed put. "What's in my mind?" he said. "Well, one thing in my mind is this. The chap's dead. And you and I are the only people who can be involved."

"But neither of us is." The stranger was suddenly impatient. "I know nothing about the matter whatever. As you no doubt saw, I had no intention of coming up to the summit of the Tor. As for you, sir, the chance of your having contrived this"—and the stranger nodded grimly towards the body—"seems to me inconsiderable." And again the stranger smiled. He was the elderly experienced man, undemonstrative, but genuinely liking a youngster who shaped well. "Now listen. You heard a shot as you were approaching this summit from the other side?"

"Certainly I did."

"But nobody appeared?"

"Nobody."

"And you saw nobody on this skyline—here where we are standing now?"

David shook his head. "No. But one wouldn't, unless they came close to the edge. Study the lie of the place, and you'll see."

"You're perfectly right." The stranger said this after a careful survey both of the rocky basin in which they stood and of the entire terrain beneath them. "Now, where were you when you heard a shot?"

David pointed out what had been his approximate position. For the moment he was quite prepared to let the stranger take the lead. He had a notion that, if he kept wide enough awake, it might be a way of learning something. "And then I came straight up," he said.

"Very well. And you can see that, on either hand, the summit falls away on a perfectly bare shoulder of moor. There's nothing remotely approaching continuous cover. Of course there's the next tor—the Loaf, I think it's called. There is cover there. But one couldn't make it all that quickly."

David studied the terrain. He was rather powerfully aware, once more, of its loneliness. But the chap seemed right about the topography. "Yes," he said, "I agree."

The stranger nodded. "So far, so good. We can be clear that, after that shot was fired, nobody could have got away without one or other of us spotting him. You'll admit that?"

"Yes—if you were looking towards the Tor every now and then." David paused. "When I saw you, you seemed entirely absorbed in the view in the other direction."

"My dear lad, I have no doubt you hailed me within seconds of becoming aware of me. I may have been looking the other way, just then. But of course I kept glancing at the Tor, and at the skyline round it. One naturally does in country like this." The stranger was again faintly impatient. "But my main point is simply that you are right in your general reading of the situation. If you were down there and heard a shot, and if it was that shot that killed this man, then either he shot himself, or I did. Is that right?"

"Yes, I think it is."

"And you can see that somebody coming along to investigate—as the police will presently have to do—will be obliged to consider the converse possibility?"

"That if this is murder, I may be the murderer? Yes, of course." David said this steadily, although it was the first time that his mind had in fact clearly focussed on the fantastic fact that he might himself fall under suspicion.

The stranger had his kindly smile again. "But fortunately, you know, far more people blow their own brains out than have it done for them by another person. Suicide is far the most substantial probability we confront. No doubt you see that. But there's another possibility, and one which I think you haven't considered. This fellow may really have been murdered, and an appearance of suicide simply fixed on him. It's a tenable hypothesis, allowing for the possibility of your being mistaken about that shot."

"How could I be mistaken about that shot?" David asked this with a puzzled air that wasn't wholly genuine. He really was learning something, he felt. For there was an unnatural slant to the way the stranger was going to work with this police talk. He might of course be authentically cool and unperturbed. That was quite in the middle-aged, military picture. But there was something spurious in his attitude, all the same. Could he, conceivably, be playing for time? Suddenly alert to a danger he hadn't so far thought of, David strolled again to the verge of the rocky platform, mounted the low natural rampart that almost surrounded it, and took another survey of the moor. At least that was all right. There were no confederates of the stranger's drawing a sinister cordon round the summit, although they might conceivably be lurking behind the Loaf. Slightly abashed at having entertained this highly melodramatic fancy, David repeated his question. "How could I be mistaken about the shot?"

"There is, you know, a certain amount of shooting on

the moor. You may have heard shots earlier on your walk. Then, finding this"—and the stranger gave his curt nod again at the body—"your mind may have played a trick on you. Or there may have happened to be a shot quite far away, which your ear just caught. Then, when you came on a man with a bullet through his head, your memory brought the sound, so to speak, to close quarters."

"I'm not sure I see what you're getting at."

"That's how you may feel in court."

"In court?" Despite himself, David was startled.

"If this awkward business ever gets there. Counsel have a trick of going ahead so that it isn't easy for the witness to see their drift. It can be unnerving."

David felt rather cross at this. "I don't think," he said, "I'm very interested in that at the moment."

"Very well—and what I'm trying to say, then, is this: granted that any shot you heard or thought you heard *wasn't* in fact the shot that despatched our unfortunate friend here, he may have been murdered—but murdered well before either of us came on the scene."

"The body's warm."

The stranger shook his head. "I'm not conjecturing that this happened last night. The inside of an hour is all we need. If the police take it into their heads that this isn't suicide—and I can't see why they should—there would be a perfectly reasonable line in that."

"I see." And—if rather obscurely—David thought that he *did* see. The stranger was feeling his way—and in a direction decidedly less than honest. "What about the smoke?" David asked abruptly. "I suppose you saw *that?*"

"Yes, I saw the smoke." Very surprisingly, the urbane stranger flushed. It was almost as if he had been stung to some sudden anger. Then he turned away, walked to the little heap of ashes, stared at it, and stirred it with his toe. "Odd, no doubt," he said. "There's nothing up here that could catch fire by any sort of accident. Somebody carried up the materials for a little fire."

"A signal, perhaps?"

"A signal?" For a moment the stranger looked quite blank. "Well, that's an idea. I hadn't thought of it." He smiled. "I see you have a romantic imagination."

"Isn't it the significant point that a dead man can't light a fire? And a tiny fire like that couldn't keep going for very long."

The stranger made a gesture of agreement. "That's no doubt true. But it's again just a matter of timing. Neither you nor I had the approaches to the Tor very securely commanded for long before you got here. When you look out over the moor from this point, you get the impression that there's no possible cover for miles. But that's an exaggeration. If you gave me fifteen minutes, I could make myself invisible even to a fellow with binoculars. And I believe I could manage it either north, south, east or west."

David thought that it was his turn to show a little impatience. "Look here," he said, "I'm not really sure we're getting anywhere. Hadn't we better decide what we're going to do?"

"Quite right. And the answer, of course, is get help— not that help means much to our friend here. One of us had better stay put, and the other make for the nearest village. I don't think it matters which way we decide."

David was silent for a moment. Perhaps it was instructive that the stranger hadn't simply given a brisk order. There seemed to be something like an admission in it. He was no longer quite confidently claiming to be simply a senior and authoritative person who had happened to come along. "I think it does matter," David said. "Or rather, I don't think your suggestion will do at all. If a

44

policeman dropped down on us this minute, he'd be quite clear he mustn't lose sight of either of us. Well, it's the same just with ourselves. We must either stay here together until we can attract attention, or we must keep each other company to the nearest village."

The stranger was silent for a moment, as if considering these propositions impartially. Then he shook his head. "From my point of view," he said, "all this is nonsense. I know I didn't shoot this poor devil, and I have a quite simple certainty that you didn't either. It's clear he blew his own brains out, and that's the whole thing. But I don't like the notion of our both abandoning his body. There's something indecent in it. And simply waiting for somebody to turn up is out of the question. We might be here for hours—indeed for days."

"There's no point in arguing," David said. "You may as well know that I don't mean to lose sight of you until we're both in the presence of the police."

6 IT MARKED A stage. They looked at each other. David's hands had been in his trouser-pockets, but now he took them out. They were handier that way. He tried to remember such modest instruction in unarmed combat as the Army had seen fit to give him. He didn't recall much more than it was a nasty field of knowledge.

Not that the stranger appeared dangerous. He turned away and took a little stroll towards the body and back, with an incongruous air of one merely concerned to enjoy the mild sunshine. "Aren't we getting this a bit wrong?" he presently asked. "Can't we take it that we've both stumbled on this affair—and realise that there's nothing at all we can do about it? The man's dead. We can't help him in any way. Getting involved in some elaborate police-enquiry will be highly disagreeable and inconvenient. I don't know who or what you are; but at a guess I'd say you are an undergraduate on vacation. Well, this business is likely to mess up things for you for weeks. And the same consideration applies to myself. So why not just walk off—you in one direction and myself in the other? There's no conceivable means by which we can be pitched on."

David, although he had expected pretty well anything,

was aware that he must be staring at the stranger round-eyed. The man's speech had been the most complete give-away that could be conceived—and yet he appeared to be utterly unaware of the fact. There had already been hints of an attitude that was distinctly what Timothy Dumble would call off-white; and now here was a proposal utterly at variance with the character in which the stranger had begun by presenting himself. Gentlemen of military cut, who take a glance at violent death and murmur some shibboleth like "Bad show," don't propose to bolt from it fifteen minutes later. David now had no doubt that he was dealing with a complete crook. The gentleman before him was a criminal and an enemy.

This simplified matters. David presumably took no pains to conceal the conclusion to which he had come from appearing on his face. The stranger, as if belatedly conscious of crisis, had turned pale; and David could sense his body as taut and waiting. He really was dangerous now. And there was something—David felt his mind reaching for it—that he mustn't be let do. There was some simple physical action that he mustn't be allowed to take.

What the stranger did was once more to turn and stroll away. This time he moved to the periphery of the rock, so that for a moment David wondered whether he was going to make a bolt for it. But he only mounted a boulder and once more scanned the moor below. "Well," he said, "the question's academic now, anyhow. There are a couple of men making straight for the Tor." He stepped down and strolled back. "Or perhaps they're girls. I'm not sure."

It seemed to David that the point was an important one. Girls are all very well, but it isn't very feasible to call upon a brace of them to collar a thug. So he moved to the edge and made his own inspection.

The moor was as empty as before.

He swung round, already knowing what he'd see. For now—too late and when he had been fooled—he had identified that simple action that the stranger mustn't be allowed to perform. It was stooping over the body and possessing himself of that gun. There was going to be another corpse.

And of course it had happened now. The stranger was straightening himself as David turned to him, and the weapon was in his hand. There couldn't be much doubt about what he intended. Then, quite unexpectedly, he spoke. "Look at this," he said, and took a step forward, holding out the pistol—which seemed very small—as if for inspection.

This time David tumbled in a flash to what was happening. The stranger did mean murder—a second murder—and not consultation or parley. But this gun was a miserable affair, not fit for much more than *crime passionnel* in a boudoir. It would be reliable only at very close quarters indeed. And that was what the stranger was trying to make sure of now. David didn't propose to oblige him. He needed almost miraculous speed—and some adequate internal chemistry gave it to him. In an instant he was over the lip of rock behind him. There was no time to discover whether this was a possible point at which to descend; he simply had to let his toes and fingers feel for what they could find. Bare stone scraped his chest; a fragment of stone whipped past his ear and he heard a bang from above; he had just realised the incredible fact that he had really been fired on when he felt his feet touch ground. For a moment he couldn't believe this either; it was impossible that he should have come down that short but formidable descent in just no time at all. But it was true. He turned from the face of the rock without looking up, and took to his heels down the steep slope of the Tor.

There was another bang. It came just after he had felt a queer jar in one of his feet. He wondered whether his pursuer had scored a lucky hit. They said you sometimes didn't feel the pain for quite a time. But he was continuing to run all right—and now he heard nothing but the sounds of his own flight. It was ignominious. Still, he was retreating in fairly good order—very literally watching his step on this treacherous ground, and using his wits about the best course to choose. At the same time he was extremely frightened. The thought passed through his mind that it wasn't in the least like any feeling he'd experienced in Timothy's car the night before. Yet his present danger must be much less, for the stranger's pistol was next to useless to him at this range, and he himself had a lead that an elderly man wasn't at all likely to reduce, even if he attempted pursuit at all.

Making sure that there were no pitfalls for a few yards ahead David glanced over his shoulder. He hadn't done the fellow justice. He must have got down from the rocks quite as quickly as David had; and now he was coming on with what one could see at a glance to be an athlete's movement. David speeded up. At the same time he found himself doing odd sums: calculating the square miles of actual solitude available in this part of the world for the fantastic hunted-man affair he seemed to have become involved in; calculating the stranger's age and correlating it with his likely stamina.

And slowly—so that he must have covered several hundred yards during the process—David's unworthy funk did a little drain from him. He had nothing to be afraid of now except carelessness or bad luck. A heavy tumble, a twist of an ankle, and he was done for. But if he was so soft that he was actually overtaken by his pursuer in a straight race, then he just deserved whatever came to him.

He looked back again. The stranger had neither gained nor lost ground. He seemed to be fumbling in a pocket as he ran, so that David wondered if he were reaching for cartridges to reload his beastly little pistol. Then the stranger put his hand up to his mouth and blew a shrill blast on a whistle.

It came to David chiefly as outrageous, as enormous cheek. It was what a policeman would do if you snatched a fellow's watch and ran. Yet it was the stranger who was a criminal—and a criminal of the lethal sort. David looked ahead. The moor fell away from him in gentle undulations, and in the distance he could just distinguish a line of posts. On every fourth or fifth post there would be a hawk . . . The memory seemed to represent security—and indeed he knew that a couple of miles along that track there was a metalled road and then a village. At the moment, he had only to go straight ahead.

Suddenly, he realised that this was just what he couldn't do. That whistle had effected something. Dead in front of him, although several hundred yards away, a man seemed to have risen up out of the moor. And there was no mistaking his movements. He had answered a summons to join in the pursuit. The chase, David realised at once and grimly, took on a different character instantly. Two to one. That made it hare and hounds.

7 IT WAS NONSENSE, David told himself as he swung sharply to his right. To come upon a crime of violence, hard on its commission, was in itself an unlikely adventure enough. Still, such things did happen; and one man had pretty well the same remote chance of becoming involved as another. As far as the theory of probability went, David had, so to speak, nothing much to complain of. It was like winning a lottery at very long odds, or gaining some vast sum on the Pools; there was nothing in it to be surprised at. That was what Pettifor, no doubt, would point out with his easy lucidity if the matter was put to him.

Keeping a wary eye on his new antagonist, David found himself irrationally disposed to laugh as he ran. Whether this meant that he was further recovering from his funk, he didn't know. What was laughable was the spectacle of his own mind continuing, in this queer exigency, to function in the fashion of a serious reading man's. The only probability he should be concerned with at the moment was whether they were going to get him. If this second chap had a gun too, and if they were absolutely out for his life, then the prospect wasn't too good.

Again he made a quick swerve. He had just spotted an unhealthily green area in the moor in front of him. They order these things better in the highlands of Scotland, he thought. There you get large stretches of moor just right for this sort of thing, and very little of it boggy. . . . He heard a shout behind him. Presumably the stranger now felt himself within hail of his assistant, and was bellowing some instruction. And it *was* nonsense. That was what he had been telling himself. Stumbling upon a murderer strolling away from his crime was one thing; finding that he had an accomplice lurking in the middle distance was quite another. It removed the whole affair into a realm of the wildly improbable. . . . At this point in his reflections David allowed his flying feet to take a false step, with the result that he went head over heels in heather.

He picked himself up, uncomfortably breathless, and heard a further shout, now alarmingly close behind him. He ran on—and with surprising speed. There was no doubt about the state of the funk now. It had mounted again and he had the fear of death on him. For a moment, that seemed to help. He cleared a trickle of water, treacherous on its either side, with an ease that would have done credit to a gazelle. Still, he wasn't sure that his knees felt too good. Perhaps that was because of the tumble he'd taken. Or perhaps it was the funk. The important thing was to realise that life was enormously desirable. . . . He made another swerve.

This time it had been a litter of boulders that didn't suggest too good going. He was still managing to head for the road—if it could be called that—from which he had finally turned off to climb Knack Tor. But now there was a long tongue of soggy terrain dead in front of him. He remembered being told that in places there were patches of bog that could be really dangerous. Down you'd go. And after some weeks you'd begin to send up a bubble or two. But nobody would ever find you—unless, hundreds of years later, your body was dug up, perfectly preserved in peat.

That—come to think of it—simplified matters for his friends behind him. If they could just pick him off with a gun—or come up with him, David grimly added to himself, and batter him efficiently to death—then they just had to find the right sort of boggy place for him, before going comfortably home to dinner. But why hadn't they done something of the sort with the corpse they already had on their hands? Perhaps the bogs were a bit too bouncy, buoyant, sticky. Your head or your feet, say, would continue obstinately in view. An attraction for carrion crows. . . . David found his speed increasing. He realised that there was much to be said for terror. It got you along.

There was another shot. It was a feeble sort of pop, and he decided that the only firearm available to the enemy was still the pistol he had first seen in the dead man's hand. That was encouraging. He took the risk of glancing over his shoulder. There was the stranger, still hanging on, and with the second man now shoulder to shoulder with him. That was encouraging, too. He had entirely avoided being cut off, and two chaps dead behind him were no more dangerous than one. And the interval was still such that this second shot had been no more than a demonstration. Perhaps it could even be called an acknowledgment of defeat. For now the track was no distance off—and as soon as he reached it his footing would be secure as he fled. That had been their only chance, really—that he should take a second and disabling tumble. Once on a safe surface, he should be all right. The stranger had clearly been a climber, and his middle-age was of the sort that is athletically well-preserved. But David's distance had been the mile, and he didn't think he'd gone exactly flabby. Unless the second man was young and a tolerably good long-distance chap—or unless there was now some quite unlooked-for misfortune—his escape was pretty well in the bag. The realisation of this went suddenly to David's head. Without venturing to look round again, he raised one arm in the air and gave a defiant wave. There was yet another pop from the silly little gun. He brought his arm down and noticed an incredible thing. Its index finger was covered in blood.

It wasn't painful, but it was sufficiently sobering, all the same. And now, too, he had to make a sharp detour to get round that awkward tongue of bog. If his pursuers had spotted it sooner than he had—and they might have done this—then they would stand to gain quite a bit by having altered their own course first. And this would then immediately help them in another way, making it possible for them to skirt quite a steep ascent which he must take head on.

Once more David crammed on a bit of extra speed. And the rising ground proved heavy going underfoot as well, for some accident of soil or exposure made the heather on it thick and high. When he reached the top of this short rise he was glad to see an easy drop to the track, for his breath was coming shorter than, at this stage of the proceedings, was altogether reassuring. And the place really was damned lonely. There was the little track and nothing else—like a neat parting down the spine of some unnaturally well-groomed furry monster. And suddenly everything that was secure and familiar in David's life—and particularly the recent tranquilities of the George and old Pettifor, Timothy and the infant Ogg and the prosperous fishermen from Lombard Street and Westminster and Pall Mall—seemed dautingly far away. They seemed far away both in time and in space. He had a glimpse of what it would be like to lose his courage; it would, strangely enough, be quite a different thing from being in the hell of a funk. Hurtling downhill at a pace he recognised as now far too fast for prudence, he had to reason with himself about the special dimensions of the melodrama that had reached out at him. There wasn't—there just wasn't— miles and miles and miles of this, although from the top of the rise, just as from the summit of the Tor, it had been precisely this that it looked like. Let him just keep going as he was doing, and he'd be out of this brute solitude in no time.

But just how? What must he come up with in order to be reasonably secure? David had reached the track by the time this question struck him forcibly. He had remembered from his map that there was a village of sorts straight ahead. But it might be no more than a hamlet—and would there be much security in that?

Abruptly, as sometimes happened with David's mind, the answers to his questions began to come not in words but in pictures—vivid and almost hallucinatory pictures, of the kind that will sometimes create themselves in the darkness when one is on the verge of falling asleep. He saw himself frantically interrogating a group of small children on the whereabouts of a non-existent police-station, volubly explaining himself to a silver-haired vicar out for a stroll, diving—and this was the most shocking vision of the lot—frantically under a bed in the first cottage he could enter. All this was extremely ludicrous, but it did reflect one quite sober fact, worth getting clear. If there is a fellow after you with a gun, and if he is convinced that it is pretty well your life or his, the point at which you can reckon upon assured safety isn't exactly easy to hit. This bleak persuasion grew upon David as he ran.

Of course the beastly little pistol wasn't inexhaustible,

and it wasn't assured that the gentleman with the good shoes and the nicely trimmed moustache had a pocket bulging with spare cartridges. As soon as he was out of ammunition he was done for—and so was his obscurely glimpsed confederate. If David could have been sure that the last shot had been already fired, he would quite confidently have stood in his tracks now.

His conviction of this was surprising. After all, it would still be two to one, and he wasn't himself a particular star in a rough house. But it did quite unchallengeably come to him that he would get enormous satisfaction from turning round and doing his best to lay out the two of them. He was still bolting—but at this new thought he felt blood going to his head. And once more the thought turned into pictures. He saw himself deftly dealing with his pursuers so that they went down writhing and howling. This vision was so satisfactory—particularly as coming after the others —that it must have usurped upon reality for some seconds. When David, still running, returned to a proper awareness of his actual surroundings, it was to find his situation transformed. Straight in front of him on the narrow road stood a stationary car.

It was odd that he hadn't seen it sooner; and odd that, whether approaching or already arrived, it hadn't been visible from the summit of the Tor. But at once he saw the explanation. The track took a sharp dip here and ran for some fifteen yards between steep banks. The result was a particularly sheltered spot, which made a pleasant trap for the mild noon warmth. And the single occupant of the car —it was a large open car—seemed to be making the most of this. It was a young woman. She was reclining lengthwise on the front seat and contentedly eating a sandwich, while at the same time exposing to the gentle influence of the sunshine a generous stretch of bare legs which were already unseasonably brown. It wasn't exactly an elegant spectacle; but even in his extremely preoccupied situation David was faintly aware of it as a pleasing one.

The girl turned her head and stared at him. That was natural. Pounding down this lonely track in a state of near exhaustion, he must be a puzzling, if not positively an alarming spectacle. But what on earth was he to do? This hadn't been one of the imaginary situations lately mirroring themselves in his mind. It contained quite a new element, which it took him only a second to identify. He himself wasn't merely in danger; he was dangerous. In this isolated place, and with those two thugs still after him, he just wasn't healthy to associate with. If the young woman had been a young man—or even an infant like Pettifor's bearded nephew, Ogg—it would be different. It would be fair to make another chap take his chance. But you couldn't very well ask a girl to join you as a target even for the silliest little pistol. It wouldn't be the thing at all.

As David was revolving these commonplace chivalric notions the girl rapidly withdrew her legs from view and then spoke. "Can I help you?" she asked.

It was a comically incongruous question—the kind with which somebody advances upon you in a shop. Not that the girl seemed out of a shop; she was what David with his large and innocent social assumptions thought of as an ordinary sort of girl—meaning the sort he commonly met. Well, he had met this one; she had uttered; and there was one plain point that must be decided in a split second. Either he must say "Yes" and stop, or "No" and run on. He could hear no sound behind him at the moment, but in no time his pursuers would be on the road and almost within range again. There certainly wasn't leisure for what could be called conversation. "No," he said. "I'm quite all right."

And he ran on.

The thugs wouldn't, he supposed, sock her as they passed. At least she had a better chance of being left entirely out of it than if he had started explanations and asked her to drive him to the nearest town. But here, he saw, had been a problem that might recur. A gaggle of old women, for instance, would have to be given the same answer. He ran on. And then he heard the car's engine start to life behind him.

He hadn't thought of that. She was curious, or intrigued, or genuinely concerned. And here she was. He hadn't covered a further fifty yards before she was slowing down just abreast of him. This time he did halt. There was nothing else to do. And the halt told him how fagged he was. He could, he supposed, tell his legs to get going again. And they'd probably obey. But they wouldn't like it, all the same.

"Are you running away from something?" The girl looked straight at him as she asked this. Her eyes were a deep, deep blue. She seemed seriously puzzled.

"Yes—I am."

It was a mere matter of breathing that constrained David to this brevity. He saw her look back along the road, which was still empty, before speaking again. "Are you a convict?" she asked prosaically.

He didn't know whether to laugh, or to damn her silently for an idiot woman. And even if she was a bit dumb, she was extremely good looking. But his perception of this was for the moment entirely by the way; it had nothing to do with the urgency with which he suddenly said, "No, I'm not—I promise. But I've got to get away, all the same. Will you take me?"

"Yes, certainly. Get in."

He was beside her in a flash. Granted that they could

get away instantly, he was convinced he had taken the right course. Once they were travelling, she could be in no danger at all, and no more could he himself—which, after all, remained a consideration of some moment. But to leave her in his wake, so to speak, by taking again to the moor, or to go on down the road and have her tagging along making helpful noises, was to expose her to at least some unknown degree of risk. "Drive straight on," he said. "And then I'll begin explaining."

The girl nodded, and tugged at the starter. David was conscious of a sudden fresh anxiety. He hadn't noticed that she'd stopped the engine. Still, it was a big modern car, and there oughtn't to be any trouble. But, for the moment, the engine didn't fire.

"Damn." The girl was aware of trouble. And she wasn't looking at the controls, although her hands were moving over them confidently. Her eyes—those really lovely eyes —were fixed on a driving-mirror on the wind-screen. "Is that them—the people who are after you?"

David turned and looked back along the road. His pursuers were further back than he had expected, and only just identifiable. There could be no doubt of them, all the same—and they were coming along hard. "Yes," he said, "that's them." And he added; "Are we going to go?"

"Of course we're going to go." The girl spoke sharply. "The carburettor floods a bit, if you muck it. And I have, I'm afraid. But we'll do it—with seconds in hand. Only we must give it a few seconds now."

"All right." David spoke as casually as he could. He felt that, after all, he had done quite the wrong thing. "But they're not very nice people, I'm afraid. If the worst comes to worst, will you lie down in the car when I tell you to?"

"Yes—if it will ease your mind." The girl's voice was cool and faintly ironical so that he guessed she'd not easily

59

lose her head. But her body was tense, and her hand hovered over the starter. She might have been counting. "Now," she said, and pulled. "Damn," she said. "Damn, damn, damn!" The engine had turned over, and again nothing had happened.

David looked back. It wouldn't do. The position, in fact, was desperate. He had involved this thoroughly commendable young woman in disgusting danger after all. And now she was looking at him inquiringly, so that their eyes met. And instantly he was moved by some quite inexplicable prompting—an instinct, a perception, a calculation: he didn't know what. "I'll go," he said. And he jumped from the car and ran.

Of course they wouldn't pause to hold any reckoning with the girl; there would be no conceivable sense in that. Indeed they would probably deviate from the road in order to avoid her, and he would himself gain quite a number of yards as a result. There could be only one reason why the stranger was persisting in this desperate pursuit: he just couldn't risk David's getting away and being in a position subsequently to identify him. And his whole instinct would be to avoid the observation of anybody else. He would certainly give the girl—and whatever other casual wayfarers might come along—as wide a berth as he could.

So David ran on with a tolerably easy mind, and with an imagination less inclined to extravagant flights about the immediate future. They couldn't, surely, follow him into even the most miserable hamlet, because as soon as they attracted any sort of notice the whole basis of their present operation lapsed. And it was impossible that he now had far to go. The track was rising steeply before him, and he guessed that when he reached the top he would look down a corresponding slope upon a scatter of chimneys and roof-tops perhaps no more than half-a-mile away. He'd certainly make that. For he had been wrong about his legs. They were still not in the least indisposed to do just what he intended them to. He shortened his pace to cope with the gradient and went up it not too badly. And sure enough there was the little village, in full view below. Beyond it he could see fields and trees. He had got to the verge of the moor.

Well, he never wanted to see it again. Remembering to think about his breathing, he opened out a bit, as he might have done at the end of a big cross-country effort. And then, behind him, he heard a car. It sounded as if it was coming at a great speed, although the road certainly wasn't a good one for fast driving. Indeed it wasn't much of a road for motoring at all—a fact that had made the presence of the girl rather surprising. But no doubt it cut off a corner of the moor, and got a certain amount of traffic on that account.

David glanced over his shoulder as he continued to run. But the brow of the hill he had just come over cut off his view, and the car was almost upon him as soon as it was visible. It wasn't an unknown car; it was the girl's. She must have got it going after all, and be proposing to make up for its previous failure by coming on rapidly to pick him up. David drew to the side of the road, halted and turned. It was only then that he had a full view. And he saw that it wasn't the girl who was driving. It was the stranger.

The next seconds were completely confused. The car swerved on the road. David was just supposing that the stranger's pace had caused him to lose control of the steering when he found himself acting in a way that seemed utterly uncontrolled itself. Entirely without conscious calculation, he had flung himself off the road and head over heels down a gentle slope that flanked it. There was a roar in his ears, and heather whipped his face as the wheels missed him by inches. He scrambled up, breathless and bewildered. The car was thirty yards ahead, stationary and canted over in what seemed a shallow ditch. The stranger and another man were climbing out. There was no sign of the girl.

For an instant the affair took, for David, one of its unpredictable dips into the ludicrous. His assailants, heaving themselves to the ground after just failing to bring off another murder, looked merely absurd, like unfortunate minor actors compelled to hazardous roles in some slapstick comedy. But if this persuasion suggested that David had gone a bit light-headed, the attack fortunately didn't last. He got himself on the road again—which was something the car didn't look likely to manage—and ran.

He ran, rather faster than he had yet run, back the way he came.

8 FOR THERE WAS something he must discover at once. Had they merely tricked that girl, or had they used violence? In either case, his own encounter with her had been unfortunate, to say the least, and he owed it to himself to investigate. Anyway, the thugs were now between him and the village, so there was nothing that could be called quixotic in his changed direction. It was true he hadn't a great deal more running in him—but there wasn't the slightest reason to suppose that his enemies had either. He turned and took a look at them as he made once more for the brow of the hill. If they proposed to come after him, they hadn't yet got down to it. They were still standing beside the car, and the stranger seemed to be rubbing or feeling his leg. With any luck, they'd both got a much worse jolt out of the late proceedings than David had.

He was back on top of the rise, and for a moment he thought he had spotted the girl, walking towards him a little more than two hundred yards away. But it wasn't the girl. It was a man.

David stopped. He was discovering that he didn't any longer like men. He distrusted them. And particularly when they were equipped with firearms. Perhaps this man wasn't. But perhaps he was. David could see something under his arm. It might be a fishing-rod. It might even be no more than a walking-stick. But there could be no doubt that it might be a gun.

The man was sauntering down the road. If he had seen David, he gave no sign. He was tall. He was in knicker-bockers—and already you could guess that these garments, although rural, were not rustic. A country gentleman, you would say. . . . At this point it was revealed to David that he had come to dislike gentlemen even more than just plain men. He suspected the figure advancing upon him of having another well clipped moustache and a disposition to murmur that this was a good or that was a bad show. And now he was certain of what was under the chap's arm. Or rather he wasn't. Probably it was a shot-gun. But it might very well be a rifle.

The man—gentle or simple—steadily advanced. Some-times he looked to his right and sometimes to his left—as if, David thought, in some hope of a hippo or a tiger. What he didn't seem to do with any intensity or even in-terest was to look ahead. Already David felt himself being rather pointedly ignored. And this, somehow, was an atti-tude he didn't at all like.

He tried to take hold of himself and make some contact with common sense. It was really inconceivable that here could be another of them. Since he left Nymph Mona-chorum that morning the English countryside couldn't suddenly have been given over *en bloc* to desperadoes. The vast probability was that this approaching figure was harmless. And that was to put it too mildly. Here, almost certainly, was a law-abiding citizen—but one, happily, who was at the moment bearing arms. Whether rifle or shot-gun, his weapon could certainly give that idiotic little pistol points.

David moved forward again. As he did so, the advancing figure took his gun from under his arm and appeared casually to examine it. That ought to be all right. But for some reason it wasn't. David, although not particularly expert at that sort of thing, felt there was something wrong with the approaching sportsman and his actions. And there was now not much more than a hundred yards between them. That made him, he supposed, already a sitting target for anybody who knew one end of a rifle from another.

Clearly he must do his best to find the girl as soon as he could. That was only common decency. But, even if he could get around this fellow in knickerbockers, he wouldn't be in much of a position to help. Supposing no harm had come to her yet—which remained the substantial probability—it might be disastrous to lead these fellows back to her. In fact his only reasonable course seemed to be immediate evasive action. If he was wrong about the man in front, and that action robbed him of a perfectly respectable potential ally—well, it was just too bad.

David looked behind him. His first enemies, he saw, were now on the move again. He looked to his left. Here, on the edge of the moor, there was really a good deal of cover: broken ground with here and there a thicket or a spinney, running down to a shallow valley in which a stream appeared to run through long, narrow plantations. David swung round and raced for a promising little gully he had spotted no farther off than a stone's throw. Something whined past his head. He thought it must have been an insect close to his ear—until a fraction of a second later he heard a crack behind him.

Well, he hadn't been wrong. Doubling up and racing as he hadn't raced before, he told himself there was some satisfaction in that. But there was small satisfaction in anything else. A rifle—even a light sporting rifle—entirely altered the complexion of things. In skilled hands it meant nothing else than quick death—or it certainly meant that if he were driven back towards the open moor. His best chance lay in taking substantial risks in order to work rapidly round to the village. They couldn't—they just couldn't—pursue him into that with guns blazing. This that he'd strayed into wasn't a 3-D western. There was—there just must be—in every sense a limit to how far they could go.

The next stage of David's flight was curiously unsubstantial and shadowy. His brain didn't seem to have much control of it. And yet it wasn't blundering or precipitate. Indeed what it now for the first time chiefly required was a great deal of wariness and calculation. The terrain—almost before his noticing it—had entirely changed; he moved behind the cover of high earthen dykes, crawled through thickets, lay listening in a ditch for sounds that didn't come.

Slowly he realised that—perhaps just by letting something primitive to the point of mindlessness take over—he had shaken off his pursuers entirely for a time. He didn't know for what sort of time, because it was chiefly his sense of time that had gone queer. What he did sharply retain was a sense of direction. He knew just where that village was. Over a field, up the stream, round a bend, and there it would be. Indeed he could see what must be the first of its cottages, white-walled and grey-thatched, just where the stream wound out of sight. It was hard not to believe that he had a clear road to safety. There were sheep in the field; he could hear a dog barking; and from a direction hard to fix there came the low throb of an engine—he supposed it must be some sort of pump. His enemies seemed to belong to a past he couldn't very clearly remember. Probably they had gone home to tea.

It was when he caught himself with this childish thought in his head that David realised the possible danger of a treachery within. Quite suddenly he had become rather shamefully fagged out. That was it. If he wasn't careful, he'd simply be sitting down in the middle of that field and counting the daisies. Chaps like that don't go home to tea. As soon as you give them the slip, and they can't any longer actually come pounding after you, they start thinking ahead. They start doing your thinking for you. That means they know it's the village there that you're trying to make. So they form a screen before it.

Crouched by the side of the gate, peering cautiously into the utterly peaceful field beyond, David told himself he hadn't got that quite right. It was almost a certain bet that they were indeed between him and the village—but, after all, there wasn't a whole troop of them. They couldn't be, as it were, manning a line. They would be at vantage points. And they'd give him credit by this time for a good deal of cunning and caution. They'd be watching the tricky approaches, the clever ways in, the sequences of adequate cover one used to be made to trace out on field-days. So the best thing to do would be to get up and walk straight and openly ahead.

David stood up. The visible scene for some reason rather swam before him, but he was solemnly sure that his muzzy head had really evolved a masterpiece of tactics. He clambered over the gate—it was something he would have vaulted earlier in the day—and marched diagonally across the field. He found himself counting the sheep. That was masterly, too. It kept you awake. Or was that what it didn't do? He was across the field. And—as he had been so rightly confident—nothing whatever had happened.

It was a nice stream. It clucked and burbled. The pulse

of the engine was louder. It would be pumping water up to cattle-troughs. All this was settled country—farmers, shepherds, barking but friendly dogs. And here was a cottage. He would go in and explain himself. The people might be surprised. But he would make everything perfectly clear.

He was inside the door of the cottage—a solid two-storey building—before he realised that there wasn't in fact a door there. Nothing, that was to say, you could shut. There was just the doorway. The cottage was abandoned and partly ruined. He remembered there were a lot like that, often scattered in rather isolated positions about this countryside. Some change in its rural economy had resulted in a sort of abandoning of outposts. You got the same effect, he remembered, in the fens—right at the other end of England. Cottages disintegrating and sinking into the soil. Not because of a declining prosperity, but because of buses and motor-bikes. The effect was very dreary, all the same.

David knew that these were desperately irrelevant thoughts, but for a few seconds he continued to wander over rotten floor-boards amid a smell of damp. He tried to remember what the stuff was called—the stuff places like this were built with. Cob—was that it? He stopped and listened. The stream clucked. Just a sort of clay and gravel. Probably a discovery of primitive man hereabouts, and chaps had gone on building that way ever since. It would be very good stuff for stopping a bullet. . . .

The derelict cottage was suddenly unfriendly, even sinister. He wondered why. It was something about stopping bullets. David went out into the open again and walked upstream. There was a little path, and farther on he could see another building, with signs of a road or track leading away from it. That would take him straight into the village. He had—he reflected without alarm—rather lost grip of things during the preceding few minutes. But he was quite on top of them again now. There was this plan of walking openly and straight ahead. Because the enemy would be looking for somebody lurking and skulking. That was it. And he had almost won through already. He could hear children's voices, faint but indubitable, from somewhere dead in front of him.

Now there was a road—in bad repair, but quite capable of taking a car or lorry. It made a loop to take in this other building, which was now straight before him. He could see no sign of life in it either, and he remembered there would be no point in going in and wandering about. But it was an odd building, small but of complicated design, as if built for some technical purpose. The stream ran past it—or rather through a wing of it, as if it were some sort of mill. David was curious about it. And so, he noticed, was somebody else. There was a man standing looking at it. David remembered he didn't like men. And then he saw that this was one of the men he particularly didn't like. It was the man in knickerbockers.

Only the length of the building separated them. The man turned round, and their eyes met.

9 THE SUDDENNESS AND directness of this encounter quite woke David up. He ceased to believe he was on top of things. He accurately estimated the largeness of the probability that in a few minutes he would be dead. And this contemplation of mortality was enlivening. He made a dash for the shelter of the building. Not that it felt like dashing. His sensation was of having been launched from a catapult. Anyway, for the moment he had gained comparative safety.

This building too appeared to be deserted and derelict. He was in a bare, square room with a concrete floor punctured here and there by broken and rusted iron pipes; and in one corner a cast-iron spiral staircase mounted through a square hole in the ceiling. On one wall there was an array of switches and fuse-boxes suggesting some quite elaborate electrical installation, but the wiring had been ripped away as if somebody had gone through the place in an insane resentment. All the windows were broken, and in the middle of the floor were the remains of a large cask which appeared to have been battered to pieces. On a door leading to some further room there flapped a printed notice about minimum wages in the cider industry. It was all acutely dismal, and David revolted against the notion of ending his days in it. He ran to the spiral staircase and climbed.

It turned out that this was a hazardous action in itself. The staircase clearly suffered from a badly fractured spine; it swayed alarmingly as David went up; and when he reached security on the next storey he was prompted to turn and give it a vicious kick. It went down with a crash, and dust and rust rose in clouds about him. There would have been great satisfaction in the spectacle of the staircase's coming down on the man in knickerbockers. But he didn't seem yet to have appeared on the scene. And David couldn't hear anybody moving. The only sound was of a motor-bike engine, growing fainter on a road that couldn't be very far away. This wretched little failure of a factory—if that was the word for it—couldn't really be remote from the fringes of civilization.

This room was much like the one below. But on one side it had an open archway leading to another derelict room a good deal larger; and opposite this there was a big opening which gave on a narrow cement platform jutting out into open air. Above this hung the remains of a derrick, which meant that the set-up must have been for loading or unloading lorries down below. The adjoining room contained some large chunks of abandoned machinery; and there appeared to be both a substantial staircase and the remains of a lift or hoist at the far end. The room David found himself in had nothing but hundreds—perhaps thousands—of small, empty bottles. These were stacked in crates, or piled, broken and unbroken, on the floor. Many had labels, and David picked one up mechanically and looked at it. It seemed that the bottle had contained, or been destined to contain, something called pineapple nectar. A shameful end, he thought, for honest apples. The nasty little place deserved its failure. David was about to drop the bottle when he heard a sound in the farther room, and swung round. There was the stranger's assistant—the fellow who had sprung up out of the moor. He was just emerging from the staircase at the far end, and was already visible from the knees up. He didn't seem to be carrying any sort of gun. David flung the bottle as hard as he could at this displeasing figure, and it smashed on the wall immediately behind his head. The man ducked, sank and vanished. It was one up to pineapple nectar.

David grabbed another bottle and ran to the open platform. The road, as he had guessed, ran directly below. On its other side, leaning against a low stone wall with a great air of quiet musing, was the man in knickerbockers. He was smoking a pipe, and his gun wasn't visible. He looked up. It was the second time his glance had met David's. The man in knickerbockers looked, but didn't move. There was something extremely offensive about this, and David instantly took a shy at him. It wasn't a very good shot, but the bottle did at least catch the chap on the knee. He gave a yelp, and seemed to reach for something concealed behind the wall. Then he thought better of this and simply stayed put, keeping a wary eye aloft the while. David couldn't afford the luxury of having another go. He swung round again.

The other man had reappeared. This time he was clear of the staircase. But there was no sign of his boss; and David had a notion that, left alone, he wasn't too keen on his job. But he was advancing at a run, so it seemed an ugly moment, all the same. David had nothing but the bottles. The trouble about flinging bottles is the difficulty of keeping up any sort of quick-fire action. David grabbed a whole crate of them and lobbed that. It wasn't much of an idea, and hardly deserved the success it achieved. The crate flew to the ceiling and produced a very good imitation of a fragmentation bomb. Bottles rained, alarmingly if rather harmlessly, on the enemy. And the man, with a lack of tenacity which confirmed David's impression of him, once more retreated down the staircase.

For the moment, the affair had taken on a tepid character that David couldn't account for. There were no bullets flying, and this last advance upon him had been distinctly irresolute. It was almost as if his pursuers were now rather doubtful about what they could do with him if they got him. Keeping an eye on the staircase, David made another cautious move to the concrete platform. The man in knickerbockers was still negligently posed by the wall. Chiefly by way of keeping his spirits up, David sent another pineapple nectar at him. But the shot went wide, and the man in knickerbockers didn't deign to notice it. He might have been a person of philosophic inclination, pausing in the course of a rural walk to meditate upon the mutability of human affairs. But now there was a sound of footsteps, and the second man appeared round an angle of the building and joined him. The two held what appeared to be a casual wayside talk. David felt he now knew why there was no more shooting. The village with its miscellaneous populace was really just round the corner, and his friends below felt themselves to be virtually in the public eye—and within range of the public ear. The row made by the collapse of the spiral staircase must have distressed them very much. They knew that any further little murder they had on hand must now be given effect to in a quiet and unobstrusive manner. David's own line, correspondingly, was to create all the uproar he could.

Here was a purpose for which the bottles seemed simply ideal. David picked up another whole crate and sent it hurtling from the platform to the road. The racket was pretty good. Then he tried the hole in the floor where the spiral staircase had been. That was much better; the reverberation in the large enclosed space below was really terrific. He followed up with several more crates. The exercise was altogether exhilarating, and he was astonished that only a little time before he had felt pretty well dead to the world.

Then he paused to listen. Nobody had attempted to come up the surviving staircase again, but he could hear sounds from that direction suggesting that some new move might be going forward. But presently these fell silent again, and he made another survey of the road. The two men were conferring together once more—and this time with what was a distinctly uneasy air. Still, they were sticking to their post; and the heroic row David had contrived didn't appear to have alerted the neighbourhood. This was disappointing. He doubted whether he could step up the general effect of disturbance further; and his having made such a pandemonium without in fact drawing any attention from the surrounding countryside would surely embolden the enemy to finish their job with firearms after all. David had just arrived at this less cheering view of things when he heard a rumble from up the road.

It was a hay-wain. At least it was that if you can so describe an affair trundling along behind a motor tractor. The tractor was small and so was its driver—a lad who might have been fifteen but looked no more than twelve. But the load of hay on the wagon behind was enormous, and David had only to take one glance at it to see that deliverance had come. The boy indeed couldn't be appealed to—whatever his years, they were too tender to be put in any jeopardy—but that was a circumstance that

74

didn't matter. Within seconds the wagon was going to be directly beneath the little platform from which David was making his observations, and if he kept low he could certainly tumble into its load while secure from the observation of the two men below. It was true that they might suspect what had happened. But before they could verify this by hunting through the derelict cider factory he would be riding triumphantly into the village, as secure as a rajah in a howdah.

This last image, suddenly popping up in his picture-spinning head, so amused David that his jump when he made it was a slightly uncontrolled affair. He hit the hay all right—it would have been impossible to miss that—but contrived to wind himself to a point of quite surprising agony. He didn't, in consequence, know how many seconds, or minutes, had passed during which he took no further effective interest in the proceedings at all. He simply had a vague awareness of the wagon trundling on, and presently of a warm, dusty quality in the air that he was endeavouring to gulp back into himself. When he did recover, it was to find that his escape wasn't going entirely according to plan.

He had taken it for granted that anything moving down this road was bound to pass through the village which lay, quite certainly, no distance off. He hadn't reckoned that there might be a turning which led elsewhere. But now when he sat up and looked about him he found there wasn't a building in sight. He was being trundled along between open fields. This was discouraging. He'd had quite enough communion with nature and solitude for one day. What he wanted was a crowd.

At this stage in his reflections David got a really unpleasant shock. He thought he *heard* a crowd. This was clearly impossible; he might as well have imagined he heard the sea—which the low murmur his ear believed itself to be catching did a little resemble. The only explanation he could think of was mere auditory hallucination. He was, as they said, hearing things. And to hear things is thoroughly sinister—an aberration altogether worse than that represented by seeing things. His late adventures had unhinged his mind.

For some seconds this extravagant persuasion really held David in its grip. He then decided, very sensibly, that it would be worth considering whether there might not be some objective basis to his experience, after all. He sat up, and at once the apparently distant murmur grew louder. Moreover he now quite certainly heard another and quite different succession of sounds. Somewhere, not very far away, a rapid succession of cars was passing along a high road. And then he discovered something else. Neither this, nor the tractor chugging in front of him, accounted for all the mechanical noise he now heard. He looked behind him. The hay-wagon was being trailed by two men on motor-bikes.

10 AT THIS POINT, and for the few remaining minutes that the whole first phase of his adventure lasted, David Henchman has to be recorded as rather failing in that rôle of cool and resourceful hero which fate had for some hours so unremittingly thrust upon him. Not that he didn't presently make some quick decisions and do one or two enterprising things. There was still available in him plenty of response to challenge. Only the challenge had lost outline and definition in his head, and he was ceasing to be at all clear about what wasn't menacing.

He didn't indeed believe that the crowd he could now so definitely if unaccountably hear murmuring somewhere in the middle distance had called itself together to seek his blood. Nor did he suppose that the many cars—the tops of which he could now just see over a distant hedge—were bringing up large reinforcements of men in knickerbockers. On the other hand he just didn't pause to consider the possible harmlessness of the two motor-cyclists. He didn't reflect that they were perhaps keeping behind the hay-wagon only because it was too broad to pass on this narrow road. Conceivably Jean Cocteau's film, which had been recalled to his mind in alarming circumstances the night before, had now some responsibility for his jumping to conclusions. Certainly the men looked sinister. They were both dressed in black leather garments, with black crash-helmets and large black rubber goggles. It was impossible to tell whether they had an eye on him or not.

David crouched down in the hay again, wondering vaguely why the stuff was thus being transported about the country at this time of year. It was musty, and he was rather inclined to think that it was soporific. He had felt drowsy not long ago, when walking across a field and counting sheep. Then he had been broad awake during the battle of the bottles. And now he wasn't sure that he mightn't any moment—

Very strangely, a bell was clanging in his ear, and he sat up with a start. He thought he was back in his private school, where it was precisely in this fashion that he had been wakened in the morning. Then he realised that the clangour came from at least a couple of fields away. It was an irregular clangour—the kind produced by a hand bell rather than from any sort of belfry. At the back of his mind he knew its significance, but he couldn't quite catch hold of it. In some way it connected itself with old Pettifor, with the reading-party at the George, with that whole life which seemed aeons of time away. More particularly, the bell connected itself with Ian Dancer. Perhaps it was only that he and Ian had been at the same prepper. . . . The hay-wagon slowed down and came to a stop.

David crawled to the front to see what was happening. The boy on the tractor had risen in his seat and was staring ahead. There were two more men on motor-bikes —dead in front, this time. They had signalled the boy on the tractor to a stop. David felt a queer mixture of terror and relief. At least it wasn't a sudden bout of paranoia that had persuaded him England was suddenly teeming with his enemies. . . . Then he saw that the motor-cyclists in front were both policemen. At least they had "Police" in white paint on their crash-helmets.

David shouted. But the policemen either didn't hear him or weren't interested. There was now a good deal of noise. And then on the right, and out of the tail of his eye, David caught sight of something that he took a second to interpret: a line of coloured blobs, like children's balloons, bobbing almost simultaneously over a hedge. Somewhere there was mild cheering, but only as a background now to the pounding hooves of the advancing horses. For that, of course, was what it was all about. The murmuring crowd, the bell, the stream of cars still driving up, the motor-cycle police controlling the traffic where the course went across this road: they were all explained by the fact that some sort of cross-country racing was going forward. The local Hunt, in fact, was holding a Point to Point. That was why the bell had made him think of Ian Dancer. Ian was riding in a Point to Point to-day. Perhaps in this one.

Just in front of them, the course must cross the road. There wouldn't be a jump in such a position. So presumably there were gates. Yes, there they were—directly opposite each other, and just in front of the tractor. They had been taken off their hinges, and between them the metalled surface of the road had been strewn with bark. Presently the riders would come galloping through, talking unconcernedly to each other if they were near enough, but at the same time going hell-for-leather for the next jump. But what David wanted to go hell-for-leather for was the police. To have started shouting was quite idiotic. He must get down and run—run until he was positively behind them. It wasn't dignified. In fact it would have every appearance of being craven and ludicrous. But

David felt he didn't at all mind about appearances now. He just wanted his own skin to be quite, quite safe for an unspecified distance ahead. If the cops led him off as a lunatic—well, that would serve very tolerably. He'd been running a one-man show for hours. He'd had quite enough of it.

This was a thoroughly sensible resolution, but unfortunately David distinctly fell down in putting it into execution. Indeed he literally fell down, for in his haste to scramble from his perch he tripped and just escaped arriving on the road head-first. The result was much what it had been when he jumped from the cider factory to the wagon; at least some seconds passed in which he was too dazed and winded to do anything much. He was aware of the riders thundering by as he expected; and when he got to his feet he had to duck to avoid a riderless horse that came wide over the hedge and for an alarming moment appeared to blot out the sky. Then, as the thud of hooves faded, he heard engines starting to life. The tractor was moving again. It had been waved forward by the policemen. And as he himself staggered to his feet and ran ahead he saw that both policemen had swung their bikes round and ridden rapidly off. In an instant they had vanished in a cloud of dust—and even the trundling hay-wagon was retreating at a pace greater then he could make up on.

With a nasty feeling of disaster spreading from his brain to his stomach and his knees, David looked behind him. The two other motor-cyclists had got off their bikes and were advancing upon him deliberately, one on each side of the road. He had a dim sense that there might be an innocent explanation of this. But much more urgent was his conviction that it was the worst crisis yet. Only a couple of fields away there must be hundreds of people

—including policemen who, being on foot, couldn't vanish with a kick and a roar. Here however he was as completely isolated as he had ever been on the moor or amid the empties of pineapple nectar. And he didn't have another effective bolt in him. He was quite sure of that.

But this certainty must have been shared—he was presently to be convinced—by some guardian angel that was accompanying him through his adventures after all. For at this moment the earth shook, there was a sound like a bellows from over the hedge, and another riderless horse dropped out of the sky, stumbled, and half checked itself. Its flank brushed David's right shoulder. Out of old habit he made a grab at the reins—and then out of sheer inspiration a grab at the stirrup. The horse fortunately approved of his design. Within seconds David was galloping over the next field.

A horse, a horse, my kingdom for a horse . . . If just this had happened to Richard III, David thought, he might have got on top of things at Bosworth after all. Rescued in this way, he himself presumably cut an abject and even scandalous figure, and in a few minutes might well be exposed to the opprobrium of the entire county. This didn't worry him, but he rather hoped his performance wouldn't be grossly incompetent as well. The fact that two riders had been thrown suggested some stiff fences, and his jumping had never been up to anything much. He was coming up to his first test now, and it had all happened so quickly that he hadn't had time to think of trying to deflect his mount from the course. Presumably this was a second time round, but he hadn't a notion how many jumps there might be ahead. Anyway, this was the only one he'd take if he could help it. With a strange horse like this, the chances were certainly that he would go for six. . . . *Now*. He felt his body and his hands go forward, and then back again, automatically. It had been as easy as that. And he was actually in sight of some of the other riders in front of him. He had been looking out for an open gate somewhere. But now he felt that perhaps he should finish the course.

This, however, he didn't bring off. Something had happened to the horse. David's seat was down on the saddle and staying there. He had just told himself this meant they had dropped to a canter, when the brute once more changed its pace and trotted quietly off on a diagonal. Presumably it had suspected some indignity in the proceedings and had decided to go home. David judged he'd better concur.

It was thus that, minutes later, he was really in a crowd at last—or rather above a crowd, since he hadn't yet ventured to dismount. He'd been to such affairs frequently enough for the scene to be entirely familiar: rows of cars, resplendent or humble, which had disgorged picnickers around collations elaborate or simple; a line of bookies, who certainly wouldn't make a fortune; a few marquees: a bar with barrels of beer; sundry opportunities to buy ice-cream. The sun was still shining; the rows of cars gleamed and sparkled; people moved about with a great sense of leisure, of relaxation, as if the last thing anybody meant to do was to attach much importance to whatever had brought them together. It was all easily and utterly English. And, above all, it was as safe as houses—or as safe as estate-cars and horse-boxes and tents labelled "Committee" or "First Aid." David sat his beautiful hunter as if it was the top of the world. Like D. H. Lawrence, he wanted to buttonhole people and insist with some urgency that he had come through. He was rather disappointed that—at first—nobody paid any attention to him.

He certainly wasn't dressed for this part. But perhaps he passed very well for a groom or a stable-boy. There was nobody to recognise him—unless, by any chance, Ian was really here, and had brought any of the crowd along with him. . . . David leant forward and patted the horse's neck in what he judged to be a convincingly professional way. He noticed that his finger was bleeding again—the finger that had been grazed by a bullet during the incredible flight from the Tor. And it *did* seem incredible now; he almost felt that, if it weren't for these drops of blood, he would find it impossible to believe in the whole thing: that there had ever been a dead body, or a man with a clipped moustache, or even a hay wagon and two sinister men on motor-bikes. In that sun-warmed saucer of stone on the top of Knack Tor he had fallen asleep and dreamed a succession of alarming dreams prompted, perhaps, by the mild dangerousness of the previous night's affair in Timothy Dumble's car.

David's mind was working in this irresponsible way when he saw somebody looking at him over the heads of the crowd. It was the man in knickerbockers.

II THERE WAS NOTHING surprising in that. The place of their last encounter was, after all, no distance away. Nevertheless here was a disappointing discovery. The dream had obstinately cropped up again.

David slipped to the ground and walked off leaving the horse to look after itself. This was an action so excessively odd that it should have attracted general notice at once; and it was a sign that his reactions to events were now really becoming blundering and extravagant. That the man in knickerbockers couldn't very well, in present circumstances, walk up and despatch him was a simple consideration that David's mind just failed to get around to. He was dominated by the sense that he hadn't yet escaped, after all; that the job, in fact, was yet to do. So he walked away in what he thought was an unobtrusive manner. Oddly enough, nobody protested—perhaps because the horse obligingly stayed put and so didn't draw attention to itself. David climbed over a rope and edged himself into the small crowd milling around before the line of bookies.

It might have been all right—he might have formed, that is to say, some reasonable design for coping with his situation—if there hadn't been another man.

David supposed the man in knickerbockers to be coming up behind him, but this man was straight in front. And quite clearly he was out of the same stable—another country-gentleman sort of thug. David didn't stop to think that this Point to Point was stuffing with country gentlemen, and that it was rationally certain that ninety-nine per cent of them were utterly authentic and uninteresting. For one thing, this new man had a close-clipped moustache—a circumstance massively suspicious in itself. For another, he was looking at David not only with concentrated attention but also with something that powerfully suggested itself as knowledge. And for yet another, he communicated an instant impression of being formidable —of being intellectually formidable. What came oddly up in David's mind as he shied away was the feeling he'd get when knocking an old Pettifor's door with the consciousness that he had a woefully inadequate essay in his notebook. David turned aside and ran. He had an impression that his old acquaintance of the knickerbockers had momentarily lost the scent, but that his new one was coming with long strides after him.

He dodged round a tent, and was vaguely aware of a large vehicle and a couple of men in uniform. There was a second tent dead ahead, with an open flap and then a screen that prevented a view inside. David bolted into its shelter, rounded the screen, and almost stumbled over a stretcher. There was a man on it, covered with a rug up to the chin. David gave a gasp. It was Ian. It was Ian Dancer.

Ian grinned wanly. He was pale, and he had a bandage round his forehead. "Hullo, you great goon," he said. "Did you see me take it?"

David stared at him stupidly. "Take it?" he asked.

"The hell of a purler. A horse crossed me at the second

bloody jump. And now the hell-hounds have got me."

"The hell-hounds?" David, although he said this on a note of interrogation, hadn't the least doubt that Ian referred to the enemy. There must be a general disposition abroad in England to have Pettifor's luckless reading-party rapidly and comprehensively eliminated.

"The ambulance chaps—and the usual apology for a doctor."

"Oh—I see." David's mind cleared a little. "Nothing bad, I hope? Collar-bone?" He had a dim memory that Ian broke a collar-bone from time to time.

"Nothing of the sort. Chipped shoulder-blade, if you ask me." Ian spoke from matter-of-fact acquaintance with these matters. "But they're always convinced, you know, that one's concussed and dangerous. They're carting me off to the morgue. The ambulance is out there now."

David nodded. He still felt dazed—just as if he had taken the hell of a fall himself—but he was conscious of some enormous and unreasonable relief. It arose, he realised, from the simple fact that he was talking. Since his long and ghastly colloquy with the man on the Tor, and his half-dozen words with the girl in the car, he hadn't had occasion to utter a sound. "Bad luck," he said vaguely. He spoke partly just for the delight of further speech, and partly because he remembered that a flow of solicitous remarks was, oddly enough, the correct English response to people tumbling from horses.

Suddenly Ian sat up. His dark eyes sparkled, and his pale face showed its wickedest grin. "I say, David—do you think I could give them the slip?"

"Just clear out?" David remembered that this was precisely what he himself wanted to do. "Would it be quite the thing?"

Ian threw back the sheet, and in consequence suffered

86

some stab of pain that set him swearing. Then his face went obstinate. If David had spoken out of deep calculation his words couldn't have had a more definitive effect. "David Henchman," Ian said, "is the best type of public schoolboy. He makes me sick. And I'm going to do my vomiting quietly elsewhere. Quite the thing! My God." He was on his feet and peering round the screen. "Damn. It's too late. Here are the ambulance chaps coming now."

"Get out under the flies at the other end." Inspiration had come to David. "And I'll take your place."

"Take my place?" Ian stared at him. "But that would be a bit steep. They'd make a row."

"Never mind the row. It's what I want. It's important." Ian's eyes rounded. "Are you all there, David?"

"Don't argue. Clear out."

Ian gave him one more look—and David remembered thankfully that he was enormously intelligent. Ian had tumbled to the fact of real, if obscure, crisis. Without a word he turned away and vanished—with just a small yelp of pain—beneath the wall of the tent. David flung himself on the stretcher and drew the blanket up to his nose. There was no time to do anything about a bandage for his head, for the entrance to the tent was already darkened. He turned his head sideways and just hoped for the best. He had a notion that ambulance men treated you with a profound disinterest anyway.

And they carried him out. The ambulance had been backed up to the tent, and its doors were beautifully and comfortably yawning for him. But even so, he thought he caught a glimpse of his new enemy. All orthodox shooting-stick and binoculars and pork-pie hat, he was striding towards the vehicle. In the nick of time, as it seemed, the doors closed on David. His muddied shoes, dangling over the end of the stretcher, were last in. Nobody had got in with him. He felt there ought to be a nurse—and, although her presence might have been fatal, he was unreasonable enough to resent the absence of this orthodox attendant.

They weren't moving. He had an uneasy sense of some conversation—even perhaps of an argument—going on outside. There were local accents—that would be the men in charge of the ambulance—and once he heard another voice that was clipped, quiet and authoritative. He distrusted it at once. He wondered whether somebody had perhaps pounced on Ian making his illicit exit, so that the row was going to come here and now. And then he heard the engine start to life, and the ambulance moved off.

David wanted to give a shout of triumph. This was better than the hay-wagon, by a long way. He had achieved a major fault in the trail, and with luck it would defy an army of men in knickerbockers to pick it up again. It was, of course, going to be slightly awkward at the other end of his journey. They just wouldn't know whether to treat him as a criminal or as a lunatic. But that didn't greatly matter. Authority would be called in, and the astounding truth would assert itself.

He lay back in great luxury and gave himself up to idle fantasy. This was no doubt reprehensible, since he ought to have been considering how most rapidly and effectively to bring the forces of the law to bear upon the grim enigma which he had been obliged to quit so unceremoniously on the summit of Knack Tor. But instead it amused him to spin himself a number of improbable pictures of what would happen when he arrived in hospital. He heard a bell ringing—already it was only faint in the distance—and knew it must be for the next race; he reflected on his own recent equestrian appearance with placid satisfaction. And when he grew tired of that he entertained himself with sundry imaginary adventures of Ian's since they had parted. It occurred to him that his horse had in all probability been Ian's too. This amused him very much. He wondered if he was light-headed. Certainly he was again ceasing to take any very accurate account of the passage of time. It might have been within ten minutes, or it might have been after an hour, that he felt the ambulance draw to a halt.

Well, that had been that. Now he must brace himself for those difficult explanations—to doctors, matrons, nurses, goodness knew what. The doors of the ambulance opened and he was lifted out. He could, of course, sit up and say something decisive at once. But he decided that he'd let himself be carried inside first. He even shut his eyes— rather in the spirit of a child who wants to save himself up a big surprise about his whereabouts.

And this was exactly what he got. The stretcher was set down. And a voice said, grimly and very unexpectedly, "You can sit up now."

In every sense, David sat up. The place wasn't a hospital—he realised that in a flash. It was all sombre brown paint, and it seemed to smell of oil lamps and ink. And David spoke his thought—he didn't at all know whether in high indignation or great fear. "I say!" he said. "This isn't a hospital. I'm sure it's not."

"Why should it be?" The same voice spoke. "After all, you're not a patient."

David turned his head. It was the new man—the one with the pork-pie hat, the binoculars, and everything proper about him. He was standing in the middle of a bare room, and regarding David with a glance that was

89

entirely serious and absorbed. He might have been wondering just where to plant a bullet. On the other hand, his thoughts might have been quite different, for he was nothing if not inscrutable.

David had the impression of other people close behind him. But he didn't turn. Suddenly he seemed to hear—with the inner ear but nevertheless as if it were quite outside his head—Timothy Dumble's voice, remarking calmly that this was it. He tensed his muscles and gathered himself for the final show. The man in front of him seemed to know he was doing this. But he just continued to watch him keenly.

"If it's not a hospital, then just what is it?" David heard a surprisingly steady voice put this reasonable question, and recognised it with some difficulty as his own.

"It's a police-station."

David gave a snort. This time it really was indignation, pure and simple. "Thank you," he said. "And I suppose you're a policeman?"

And then—in what was the most unexpected occurrence of the day—the grim man with the binoculars smiled. "Yes," he said. "I am. My name's Appleby."

12 APPLEBY. THE NAME meant nothing to David Henchman. But now he looked around him, and was constrained to believe what he was told. It was a police-station, all right. Not the most resourceful gang of crooks could fake up such a *décor*. There was a sergeant—stolid, but plainly not disposed to regard this man Appleby as an everyday event —amiably getting him a cup of tea. There was a constable who, with equal amiability, had gone off to fetch sandwiches—for David was enormously hungry. He was much more hungry than exhausted now, so that he found it hard to believe that lately he had been behaving in such an end-of-the-tether way. "Frightfully kind of you," he said between mouthfuls. "I haven't had anything since breakfast, as a matter of fact."

"And now it's nearly three o'clock." The man called Appleby offered this with what appeared to be perfect solemnity. "Still, you've pulled through."

David blushed. "You'll think me quite idiotic. But this morning does, as it happens, seem to me an enormous time off. I'd better tell you about it."

"Quite so. But I think you'll find another cup of tea in the pot." Appleby, who seemed in no hurry, turned to the sergeant. "You don't mind our being here a little

91

longer? No need for you to bother about us."

"Certainly, Sir John. You'll stay as long as you like, of course. And we'll be getting back to work." With this the sergeant vanished, taking his subordinate with him.

David was impressed. "I say," he had, "it's frightful cheek to ask. But are you the Chief Constable or something?"

Sir John Appleby shook his head. "Dear me, no. I've no standing down here at all. And I'm sure I'll never be a Chief Constable. I work at Scotland Yard."

David found himself receiving this information with a most unsophisticated awe. "Criminal investigation?" he asked.

"Yes—that sort of thing. And it involves me in queer activities from time to time. But I don't think I've ever kidnapped anybody before. I must really apologise."

"Oh—not at all." David blushed again, judging this reply to have been exceedingly fatuous. "Only, I don't see why you should have—well, bothered. I mean to say, there I was behaving like a moron with a horse, and so on. But I don't see why you should have been interested."

"But aren't you interesting, Mr.—I think you said Henchman?"

"Yes, Henchman." David's confusion grew. "I don't think I'm a bit interesting, sir. Not, I mean, as a chap, and that sort of thing. But I suppose what's been happening to me is interesting. It's not just been fooling on another fellow's horse, and then trying to get carried off to hospital on false pretences. Of course it must look like some witless joke, I know." By this time David was rather incoherent. "But I don't see why you should take the trouble to switch me from hospital to police-station because of that. Not unless you want to charge me with obstruction or disorderly behaviour or something."

Appleby shook his head. "I can assure you," he said courteously, "that I do comparatively little on those lines."

David wasn't sure why he took no exception to this elderly irony. It was something one got quite enough of from dons. Perhaps it was just that this Appleby wasn't after him with a rifle or a pistol, and that in these circumstances he felt a little verbal sniping to be neither here nor there. "You still haven't explained," he said firmly, "why you found me interesting at all."

"You were mildly interesting from the moment you appeared on young Dancer's horse."

"You know Ian!" David heard, with disapproval, a sort of inane surprise in his own voice.

"I met him before that race. My wife's people know his relations down here—who, incidentally, provided the horse. I was a little more than mildly interested when I saw that you had taken Dancer's place on that stretcher. But it wasn't until seven-eighths of you were in the ambulance that my interest became really pronounced. Take a look at the heel of your left shoe."

David did as he was told. "Well, I'm blessed!"

"Not a direct hit, I think, or the bullet would have buried itself in the leather and be invisible. A ricochet, no doubt. And at a glance—and just from that coy corner of lead, I'd say from some very small-calibre affair."

"A beastly little pistol. No good at all." David found that this was still, most illogically, a point of resentment with him. "But," he added, "the other fellow had a rifle."

"Dear me."

"And the frightful thing is, there was a girl. They stole her car, and piled it up when they tried to get me by running me down with it. I've an awful feeling they may have knocked her out, or something. I tried to get back

93

to see, but that was when the one with the rifle headed me off. And I've had another horrible idea. The girl may be the daughter of the man they killed."

"You seem to have had quite a day." Appleby spoke without emotion, but his eyes never left David's face. "What you say requires investigation. But it explains—well, aspects of your appearance when you turned up at that Point to Point."

"A chap scared out of his wits?"

Appleby smiled faintly. "Put it that you didn't appear to have been enjoying yourself. Although I expect bits were enjoyable. It's a funny thing, but they always are."

Quite suddenly, David decided that he liked this man. "I enjoyed throwing the bottles," he said. "Hundreds of them."

Appleby looked respectful. "I've never done it on quite that scale," he murmured. "And now, perhaps, if you would tell me . . . about the whole thing?"

13 DAVID'S NARRATIVE DIDN'T take long, and it was completed in Appleby's car. Its large improbability was painfully evident to him as he talked, and he even wondered whether Appleby believed a word he was listening to. Probably there was a large class of hysterical young persons, male and female, who made a business of turning up on the police with yarns of this sort. If Appleby had made any arrangements for collecting the body from Knack Tor, or for scouring the countryside for the criminals, no sign of this appeared. He had simply done some telephoning, and then they had driven away quietly and by themselves in this discreetly powerful car. Probably Appleby was considering, among other possibilities, that of a hoax or practical joke. He might even be benevolently proposing to minimise the trouble the jokers were asking for by unobtrusively denying them much publicity . . . David looked down at the heel of his left shoe and took comfort from the tiny gleam of lead. Surely nobody could believe that a practical joker would go to quite that length of petty ingenuity.

"Here's your cider factory, I suppose."

The car had come smoothly to a halt. David realised how small had been the whole terrain over which he had spent the morning scampering. "Not cider," he said. "Pineapple nectar. And there are some of the bottles. I sent one crate, you see, into the road. I'm afraid it's rather a mess."

There was certainly a good deal of glass on the road. But Appleby seemed to take David's remark in a larger context. "The extent of the mess," he said, "is the first thing to determine. We'll go on. Have you got your bearings from this point?"

"Yes, sir. I'm pretty sure that, if we go straight ahead, we come to a road on the left. It's not much more than a track, but it takes cars, all right. And the place where they had a go at me as a pedestrian can't be more than a mile ahead."

The car gathered speed again. "I suppose," Appleby asked, "that Knack Tor isn't a bad place for a really quiet chat?"

David considered the implications of this. "It's certainly that. You're invisible yourself, because the summit is a sort of shallow cup. And if you look over and around from time to time, you'd have plenty of warning of anybody coming to interrupt."

"Quite a spot for business conference of a certain sort." Appleby changed gear to take a curve. "You hadn't anything of that kind on hand yourself?"

David was startled. This was what is called an attempt to catch one off one's guard—a bit of high class police technique. And it certainly showed that Appleby continued to have an open mind. "I certainly had nothing on hand," David replied. "As I've told you, I was just doing a solitary walk."

"And that's your sort of thing?"

"Well, yes—at times. I was a bit fed up with Pettifor's lot, as a matter of fact."

"Pettifor's lot?"

David explained about the reading-party in some detail. He even told the story of the game of chicken. Appleby listened in silence, and then returned to his point. "You hadn't a business deal to put through on that summit. And there was nothing else? For instance, a meeting with a girl?"

"Certainly not." David spoke gruffly. He was much shocked and offended. But no doubt the police had to have a sexual slant on everything. And this man Appleby, although a civilised type, was plainly implacable. "The only girl in the affair, so far as I know, is the one I came on in the car—and may have landed in something horrid. And that's bad enough, if you ask me."

The logic of this last remark wasn't very clear, but Appleby appeared prepared to acknowledge it as a reproach. "One asks these things," he said. "Sometimes, you see, one gets only half a story—or less—just because a fellow doesn't want to embarrass a lady. And sometimes it's necessary to persevere—although naturally one feels it to be a poor show."

David suddenly grinned. "You talk just like my murderer," he said. "Good shows and poor shows."

"I beg your pardon?"

He had startled Appleby—which was most satisfactory. "I rather hope to hear you have a talk with him one day, sir. Poona stuff all round."

David hadn't uttered this speech before he regretted it. There was no charitable word for it. He had said something merely impertinent. But Appleby gave no sign of being offended. Instead, he was instantly on the spot. "My dear lad, of course I'm out of the ark. And so, no doubt, was this chap you had a word with up on the Tor. But he and I didn't necessarily march in two and two.

We may be animals of entirely different kinds . . . Is this our next stop?"

The man had an eye like a hawk. If he had ever been in the ark it must have been as just that. They had been travelling at speed. But he had noticed a disturbance on the margin of the road. And when the car had stopped they got out and walked back to it. "Yes," Appleby said, "this is where they tried to get you. If they'd just managed to hit you with a wing, then they could have finished you off with a spanner—or say with the jack. You might have been found tomorrow morning, and recorded as an accident of the uglier tip-and-run sort. Miles better than putting a bullet in you. Although nastier, while the bludgeoning was going on."

Not for the first time that day, David was conscious of his stomach as feeling far from nice. This was repayment for his filthy quip about Poona. "It was a bit of an escape, of course," he said coldly. "But what we ought to be thinking about, surely, is that girl."

"Ah—you mustn't suppose I'm not thinking about her." Appleby said this in his most enigmatical fashion. "And about her car. It's gone—hasn't it?"

"It didn't look entirely knocked out." David felt instantly defensive, as if his whole yarn were now being questioned. "But I doubt whether it could have been got on the road again without a bit of a tow."

"Quite so." Appleby was now prowling about, peering at the turf and heather. Sherlock Holmes stuff, David thought. He was presently going to discover a cigarette-butt compounded of one of the rarer of the fifty-seven—was it?—varieties of tobacco. "Quite so," Appleby repeated. "But then your friends appear distinctly to possess resources. That is far the most striking thing about them. Your other Poona acquaintance"—Appleby said this without a flicker—"requires a colleague. Well, all he need do is blow a whistle. That, you know, is very notable."

"I suppose it is." David was once more uneasy. This man Appleby had only to import a certain tone into his voice for the whole adventure to become grotesquely implausible. Perhaps it was that anyway.

"You abruptly change course—being very properly concerned for the safety of that girl. And what happens? Up pops another conspirator, conveniently armed with a rifle. Later, there are two men on motor-bikes. It's true that the case against them is not wholly proven. Still, the whole set-up is striking, you'll agree." Appleby paused, and appeared to note the fact that he got no reply. "You needn't sulk," he said. "I mean precisely what I say."

David was aware of his complexion as being again awkwardly out of control. "I thought," he said, "that you were meaning that my whole yarn sounds like moonshine."

"Of course it does. It may be moonshine." Appleby's openmindedness suddenly reminded David of his American friend, Leon Kryder. "But even if it is, you know, we mustn't despair. There's a great deal that the psychiatrists can do nowadays." He smiled cheerfully at David. "Shall we drive on?"

They drove on. Presumably it was part of a high-class policeman's technique to keep you guessing. David didn't at all know how he stood with Appleby—although he continued to feel that the man was probably all right. "If you mean that it really is striking," he presently ventured, "will you tell me why? I mean, about the chap's possessing resources."

"Certainly." Appleby paused—apparently for the purpose of putting down his foot with some deliberation on the accelerator, so that David realised they would be abreast of Knack Tor in no time. "One does, of course, get gangs of various sorts. There are still race-course gangs, for instance. But they don't have quite this polite touch you seem so allergic to."

David felt it was time Appleby had dropped this Poona joke. But he didn't venture to say anything.

"Winchester and New College," Appleby continued affably. "They don't contribute much at the razor-slashing level of society. Balliol men, although they sometimes get together for curious purposes, seldom whistle for each other to come lolloping up for a man-hunt. In fact, the classes of criminal activity that produce phenomena at all corresponding to your story are not at all numerous. That's my point . . . Now, would this be the hollow where you came on the girl with the car?"

Again they had come rapidly to a stop. David felt that his enquiries were going to get no further. Besides, he was now all eagerness for any trace of the girl. "Certainly it was here," he cried, and jumped out. "I expect you can tell an awful lot by just poking round."

Appleby made no reply to this. But he did poke about very thoroughly, and ask a great many questions. It was as if he had come to some aspect of the affair that really puzzled him. "At least they didn't slug your friend," he said, "and throw her into the ditch." He gave David one of his long straight glances, as if interested to see how he took this sudden brutality of speech. "But I think you said you had an idea about her?"

"Only that she might have driven the man I found dead. Suppose he had made a date, sir, for what you called a quiet chat on the top of Knack Tor. He might have had himself brought so far, and then told this girl—perhaps his daughter—to wait. She was waiting, you know. Eating a sandwich and—well, doing a bit of sun-bathing. I felt rather butting in."

Appleby didn't conceal that he found this amusing. David wondered why—and then realised that there was perhaps something funny in the notion of a young man indulging this delicate sentiment while bolting for his life. But now they were climbing into the car again. Another half-mile, and they would have to leave it and strike across the moor. It seemed suddenly odd to David that anything in the world should have persuaded him to return here. And he hadn't come back under the protection of a squad of police. There was just this middle-aged person, whose habitual employment must be sitting in a London office and sifting through the reports of more mobile subordinates. Appleby seemed to be treating the affair as if its active phase, so to speak, was securely over, and everything would now stay put until he had tidied it up. And David experienced a sharp misgiving. That was probably how you felt, if you normally dealt with criminals without stirring from some fastness in Scotland Yard. But what if the affair wasn't over at all?

David glanced at his companion. Appleby had filled a pipe during their last halt. He was puffing contentedly as he drove—and indeed his satisfaction in the process was so evident that David felt a spasm of irritation. "Has it occurred to you," he asked, "that they may still be about?"

"Your friends?" For a second Appleby took his eyes from the road to glance at David in mild surprise. "But naturally. That's rather our hope, is it not?"

"Oh." To David this was, in fact, quite massively a new idea. "It would be rather good if they were after me still?"

"Well—say both of us." Appleby offered this addendum

as if it must hold the largest comfort. "It would be a great simplification, certainly. The needle emerging from the haystack, you might say, in the hope of getting us in a nice soft place."

David was aware of silence. The car had stopped. The engine was shut off. There was a lark singing. And straight ahead stood Knack Tor, crowned with its great dark slab of rock, and with the Loaf a little to the left. David felt that things must be kept in hand. "It's remarkable," he said conversationally, "how lonely it suddenly gets out here. I was struck by it this morning."

"I dare say you were." Appleby was looking at him with what a conceited young man would have taken to be at least provisional approval. "Well, now, shall we take our stroll?"

They took their stroll. In other words, David supposed, they set out to find the body—and anything else they might encounter. Appleby still had his pork-pie hat and his binoculars. Indeed, he still had his shooting-stick. And from his button-hole—it was something David now noticed for the first time—there dangled a cardboard label, presumably indicative of some obscurely official function at the Point to Point. He had the appearance, in fact, of one walking out to inspect the course.

And that was precisely what it had been, with David himself running a very pretty race over it. But now it all appeared on a smaller scale, less remote, less formidable. Appleby—get-up, manner and all—was certainly responsible for this effect. His car, left unattended on the track, was like a confident gesture of security; the man himself, pausing now and then to admire a vista now bleakly golden under the afternoon sun, had no appearance of one proceeding to view a corpse. And presently he began to

102

take a circuitous course, so that they were making something like a sweep round Knack Tor. And the farther distance now took up only part of his attention; he stopped once or twice as if prompted mildly to botanise among the grasses and mosses at their feet. "Visitors," he said at length. "I think they've paid a little call, and left again."

"Visitors? You mean to the Tor?" David was startled. "Since this morning?"

"That's the probability." And Appleby pointed to the ground. "Don't you see?"

David was immediately astonished that he hadn't seen. The turf here was hard and springy, but nevertheless the tracks of some sort of vehicle were clearly visible. "This bit's all right," he said. "But there must be some stretches where you couldn't bring a car."

Appleby shook his head. "Not an ordinary car, perhaps. But some sort of jeep—anything with a four-wheel drive —would do it easily. That's to say, if it avoided the boggy bits. And I think it must have got close up to the Tor."

"Might it still be there, but round at the other side?"

For a minute Appleby made no reply, but simply walked on, his eyes bent on the ground. "I don't think so," he said presently. "My impression is that it came back pretty well in its own tracks."

"Do you think it may have been brought here so that . . ."

"Of course I do." For the first time, Appleby's tone sounded faintly impatient. David guessed that he didn't at all like this development. "Well, we'll get on."

They moved forward more quickly. Although the westering sun was still shining over the moor, all warmth had gone out of it, and there was a thin chill wind. Over the summit of the Tor a hawk swung, hovered and dropped —dropped like a stone destined to smash itself on the

103

brute rock. Actually, its concern must have been with something on the farther slope. On the summit there could be nothing except a human body, and a hawk would hardly concern itself with that.

But would the body still be there? Very probably, David realised, it would have gone. That could be the only meaning of the recent passage of a motor vehicle here. Nobody, unless he were a cripple, would elect to ride, rather than to walk, to the Tor, unless he had in view some definite end for which transport was required. Yes, that was it. The enemy had come back and collected the body.

David's first reaction to this notion was regrettably childish. He would have nothing to show Appleby. It was true that Appleby could no longer very reasonably conclude his whole story to be an invention. There was now too much objective evidence for that. But, after all, the body was the big thing. It was just like those beastly thugs to make away with it . . . This was certainly a foolish line of thought, and it was immediately succeeded by one equally unpresentable. If the body wasn't there—the body of a middle-aged man with a hole in the middle of his forehead—then probably David would never see it again. There would have been no point in the thugs taking the risk of coming back here and collecting it, if all they were going to do was to abandon it in some other place. If it had vanished, it had vanished for good. David would never again have to look at it. He was surprised to discover what a relief this would be.

They were now at the foot of the rock. It was just the point at which David had scaled it. Suddenly Appleby bent down and drew something out of the heather. "Ever seen this before?" he asked.

"It's my walking-stick." David stared at the unexciting

object as if it had been a vast surprise. "Of course I dropped it when I began to climb. How awfully funny that I just haven't remembered it since. It belonged to my grandfather."

"It's a good stick." Appleby stuck it upright in a tump of heather. "We'll collect it when we come down. Now up we go."

Appleby went first and David followed. Appleby climbed rather as the principal enemy had done—with a professional touch. But David was conscious that he himself made at least a better job of it than he had managed that morning. He was on his mettle—for no better reason, it seemed, than that Appleby had commended his stick. And when he got his head over the top he saw just what he hadn't expected to see again: a pair of rather good shoes, not far from his nose, and heels in air.

"Well, here it is." There was a note of satisfaction in Appleby's voice. "Not a dream, you see. You were as wide awake as you'll ever be."

David scrambled to his feet. It was a relief, after all, that the body was still *in situ*. But he saw that there was something queer about it. He had known there was something queer as soon as he had seen the shoes. . . . "It's turned over," he said.

"What's that?" Appleby swung round on him.

"The—the body has turned over. It was on its back. It's managed to get on its face."

"And it seems to have managed to get back that pistol." As Appleby pointed, his voice was grim. And it was true. There was a pistol in the dead man's hand.

David stared. "I don't think it's the same pistol."

Appleby took a step forward, knelt by the body, and with a strong careful movement turned it over. The head hung limp. There was a hole in the middle of the forehead.

David heard Appleby's voice as if from a distance. "Not the same pistol. But is it the same man?"

"No. . . . No—it's not." David's own words came jerkily. "It's the other one."

14 "THEN SOMEBODY HAS arranged us a little surprise." Appleby, who had sat down on a ledge of rock, said this unemotionally. "At least it looks like that. But we may be flattering ourselves. We mayn't have been in their heads at all."

David realised that he was being given time to compose himself. Even so, some further seconds passed before he trusted himself to ask: "You believe it's the other man?"

"My dear chap, I haven't the slightest reason to disbelieve you."

Again David was silent for a moment. He wasn't quite certain that this form of words was wholly comforting. "I mean," he said, "it seems so wildly and utterly improbable. One body up here is unlikely enough. But two successive bodies . . . and getting themselves switched round like this . . ." He broke off rather helplessly. "It's awful, feeling so—so implausible."

"Of course you may be a thoroughly muddle-headed young man." Uttering this frank sentiment, Appleby produced his pipe again with a matter-of-factness suggesting he had seen violent death before. "The one incontrovertible circumstance is that there has been a bit of ugly business on this summit, and that you are mixed up with it."

"A mixed-up kid."

Appleby stared. "What's that?"

"Nothing . . . I'm sorry. Just something people were talking about last night. It sounds as if I am muddle-headed—quite damnably."

"It's a possibility, as I say." Appleby had now got to his feet again and put his pipe aside to examine the body. "Quite dead, I need hardly tell you. And no time ago— no time ago, at all. Even if you are very clear-headed, Henchman—quite the master-criminal, indeed—I doubt whether you can possibly have done this." And Appleby tapped the shoulder of the corpse lightly as he got to his feet again. "At a guess, I'd say that you and I had made each other's acquaintance before this fellow died. And that gets several things clear for a start. All your memories of today's events may, of course, be enormously confused and utterly unreliable. When an affair like this comes along, that's a fact a policeman must reckon with at once. Tough or not so tough, you see, it's all the same. A shock can precipitate no end of muddle as soon as the individual who has received it tries to think back. People have been known to swear with absolute conviction and sincerity that they saw Jack murder Jill, when in fact what they saw was Jill murdering Jack. But this corpse, you see, was alive and kicking when you told me your story. So that does a little simplify things."

"I see." If David hadn't entirely followed Appleby's long speech, he had at least got his wits in tolerable order again—which had perhaps been the idea. "And what do we do next?"

"Confront the awkward fact that we're deucedly short of *dramatis personae*." As he made this unexpected reply,

Appleby contentedly lit his pipe again. "There's you, of course—but I honestly don't place much reliance on you."

"Thank you very much." David was now sufficiently composed to grin at this.

"That's to say, the possibility of your being what may be called a principal personage is remote."

"A master criminal?"

"That sort of thing. So what are we left with? Not the initial victim of this morning—unless, of course, you just don't know a dead man when you see one."

"He was dead all right."

Appleby nodded. "Very good. For the moment, I accept that as a fact. And here"—and he pointed to the body—"is another fact. Call him the First Murderer. He's knocked out of the cast, too. So what have we left? Only Second Murderer—meaning your friend in knickerbockers—and an obscure First Assistant Conspirator."

"The chap who sprang up when First Murderer here blew his whistle?"

"Just that. And my instinct tells me that he is most unpromising. So who else?"

David considered this. "The Death Riders."

"Meaning the two men on motor-bikes?" Appleby smiled. "Will you forgive me if I say I don't terribly believe in—well, their relevance? They came on the scene when you yourself, you know, had every reason to be exercising what one may call a vigorously stimulated imagination."

"But they stopped their bikes as soon as I tumbled off that hay-wagon. And the last I saw of them—before I jumped on poor old Ian's horse—they were coming right at me on either side of the road."

Appleby shook his head. "I'm sorry—but for the moment I shall persist in considering them mere supers. They

109

realised that races were going forward, and they proposed to find a gap in the hedge and have a look. So what?"

Thus challenged, David took a deep breath. "The girl."

"I'll give you the girl—and even, provisionally, call her the Leading Lady. But there, you see, the cast stops off. It's unpromising. I don't like it."

David took a look at this odd policeman from Scotland Yard. He continued to think he might be rather nice. At the same time he acknowledged to himself that the wholesome instinct to rebel against the elder generation was strong in him at the moment. "What a thumping lie," he said. "You like it enormously."

Appleby laughed aloud—and so spontaneously that the sound didn't seem in the least improper in the vicinity of the dead man.

"You like it more and more," David added. "Although I can't think why." He paused to consider. "I believe I rather bored you at first—myself and my whole adventure. Not that you didn't go out of your way to pick it—and me—up."

Appleby nodded, decently sober. "You are a pick-up, all right. I acknowledge it. Any unusual appearance attracts me instantly. And then, when you told your story, I wasn't terribly keen. I acknowledge that too. You had stumbled upon some nasty local crime. And I meet too many crimes. But of course I had to see you through— and give a hand in clearing things up. A busman's holiday. Not attractive. But now it's different. You're quite right."

"And what has made it different is danger?" David was rather pleased with this. It struck him as an extraordinarily acute psychological perception.

But Appleby was looking at him once more in an infuriatingly elderly way—half astonished, half amused. "Danger? Dear me no. I used to go in for it a lot. It was quite horrid—although with its fascination, I admit. But I can't say it appeals to me now. No"—and he shook his head in what seemed a drift of oddly sombre feeling—"it's not a resource that lasts, you know. Nothing really lasts, except the queer urge to make a little knowledge when one can."

"I think I know about that." David said this quite honestly. He wasn't old Pettifor's pupil for nothing. "But does this"—and he gestured, first at the dead man and then at the solitude and silence around them—"does this have anything to do with that?"

"Only in the humblest way." Appleby had knocked out his pipe, and was kneeling again by the body. "You see, when your corpse changed to this corpse, the affair ceased to be just a crime. It became a mystery. And that's something challenging our instinct to worry things out a bit. So I like it enormously, as you have very accurately observed."

David said nothing—and in the silence a lark struck up again, like a punctual sound-effect tuned in by a conscientious B.B.C. producer. Appleby was turning out the pockets of the dead man. There was something rather horrible in the sight of it. It was like an inglorious aftermath of battle, a pillageing of the dead. And then David noticed Appleby's face. It was gentle and absorbed, so that he was reminded of Pettifor when you caught him in a library, poring over a book that contained goodness knew what. To solve this business would, of course, be to make knowledge—although in an uncommonly macabre field. But how did one begin? With this problem in his head, David waited until Appleby got to his feet again, and then asked a question. "I suppose it will somehow be possible to . . . to identify this chap?"

"Identify him? I've done that already. As a matter of

111

fact, I know him quite well."

"You know him!"

"His name is Charles Redwine. We worked together once. He was my chief during the first years of the war."

David's first emotion on hearing this extraordinary statement was of simple alarm—as if the man who made it was boldly unmasking himself as a criminal. Then he became incredulous. "It's impossible!" he cried. "Of course I can't be certain he killed the first chap. But he tried to kill me, all right." He turned and stared at the corpse. "It's true he looks everything he should be. But I just can't, can't believe he's not a bad hat!"

David stopped—aware that Appleby's eyes were once more on him with their peculiar steadiness. Appleby had sprung this as another surprise, as some sort of final test. And only an astonishing self-control—David suddenly realised—had made that possible. His own eyes had been on Appleby when he had turned over the body and first looked at the face of the dead man. The shock of recognition must have been pretty stiff. But he hadn't let a muscle flicker.

"Redwine was a crook, all right." Appleby, although he spoke sternly, seemed to realise the need of being re-assuring. "In fact, it's rather satisfactory that he's dead."

"Satisfactory?"

As usual, Appleby caught David's tone exactly. "It's certainly an indecent thing to say. And perhaps even vengeful. Redwine was one of my failures. He was the biggest of them. I failed to get him into gaol."

"When he was your chief, sir?"

"Yes, when he was my chief." Appleby had walked to the edge of the rock and was gazing out over the moor. "I found out the truth about him. And then I hesitated— for twenty-four hours. It seemed incredible. I mean, it felt incredible. There was loyalty, there was decency, there was everything against it. For twenty-four hours I let my emotions in the matter get on top of my intellect—declaring there was still a faint possibility of mistake, and so on." Appleby turned round. "You have no business to hear this, Henchman. Or rather I have no business to tell it you. But the circumstances are"—he smiled—"well, exceptional."

"I shan't spread it round, sir." David said this rather stiffly.

"In those twenty-four hours the evidence—the hard core of the evidence—melted away. It was, as they say, liquidated. So Redwine was shifted to unimportant work, and then he was pensioned off. Nothing more could be done. An eye has been kept on him since—that sort of bad hat isn't forgotten about—but any tricks he's been up to he's managed to keep to himself. That he's ended like this" —Appleby made a gesture—"suggests that honourable retirement hasn't been exactly his line."

"Does this mean that what I came upon this morning had something to do with spying—that sort of thing?"

"Well, something in that target area, I've no doubt."

"With this chap Redwine as chief spy?"

"I don't know. But clearly he wasn't on his own." Appleby turned and walked back to the centre of the shallow basin of rock. "Your story shows he had at least two fellows backing him up this morning. Well, that's quite in the common run of things, as I think I was explaining earlier. If race-course toughs work in gangs, espionage people organise themselves in rings. It works a little differently, but the principle's the same. We may be confronting a ring, Henchman—or even inside one."

David was startled. "Do you mean literally?"

"Why not?" Appleby had opened his shooting stick, which somehow he had managed to bring up with him to the summit; found a crevice in the rock for its spike to rest in; and comfortably seated himself. "As I see the matter, they're bound to be pretty interested in you still."

Although he'd had a hint of this before, David now took it in rather slowly. "Here and now?" he asked presently.

"Possibly here and now. I should explain that these are almost certainly big people. Whatever they have been up to is likely to have a good deal of significance, viewed from the standpoint of the country's security." Appleby spoke briskly and not at all portentously. "This is all right by you?"

"It's all right by me." David paused awkwardly. He was much concerned to play down any lurking heroics in his strange situation. "I'm glad," he said, "I had those sandwiches and cups of tea."

15 THE SPRING DAY would soon be over. Presently dusk—and then, very soon, darkness —would descend on the moor. And Appleby's idea seemed to be to use David as a decoy. This wasn't cheerful. But at least it was exciting. David reflected that if he could just hold on to that fact he might acquit himself without utter ignominy.

And now Appleby was studying the small patch of blackened rock which was the only remaining sign of that morning's mysterious fire. "Have the ashes been blown away?" he asked. "I don't think so. Whoever killed Redwine did a bit of a tidy up at the same time."

"Do you think the first dead man—the one I found— was some sort of bad hat too? Might he have belonged to a rival show?" David didn't know whether he ought to ask questions. But he had a strong impulse to keep his wits occupied.

"I think it's certainly possible." Appleby's reply came readily. "Suppose Redwine fixed up a quiet conference with the other fellow in this retired spot. If he did, he expected possible trouble. Otherwise he would hardly have had a colleague lurking on the moor, and another patroling the track with a rifle. And then suppose that, whether by premeditation or not, Redwine committed murder. If that

115

was so, his next move is significant. He fixes the appearance of a suicide, and then simply walks away. That means that he could apprehend no danger to himself from the subsequent discovery and identification of the body. But then you came along. You hailed him, and he realised that continuing to walk away would be no good. You would certainly go after him and tackle him. So he returned to the summit and—well, discussed the matter with you."

"And gave himself away. I mean by working round to a proposition that no honest man would make."

Appleby nodded. "Quite so. But even if you'd agreed to slip quietly out of the picture he'd have been bound to have doubts about you. When you'd recovered from the shock of the whole affair, you'd possibly go to the police. And there was another sense in which he'd given himself away. Once his presence in the neighbourhood of Knack Tor was established, the notion of suicide wouldn't stand. Investigation, that's to say, would uncover him—and with all his shady past, mind you—as in some relationship with the dead man. So he decided he had to go after you with his gun too. But I expect this is mostly stuff you've already worked out."

"Well, yes—it is." David said this almost apologetically. "But I expect you've got a good deal further."

"They've got a good deal further." And Appleby pointed again at the body. "Redwine dropped out of the hunt for you—apparently leaving it to his companions—and came up here again."

"Unless he was brought back dead."

"That's a possibility, I agree. Anyway, he was killed—and his body was substituted for the first."

David shook his head. "Does that quite follow?"

"No, it doesn't." Appleby's reply was so immediate that

116

David had a fleeting notion he was being put through a sort of oral examination as an apprentice detective. "It is just conceivable that both bodies were left here by one agency in the affair, and then that the first body was removed by another agency. That makes the time-table rather tight, I feel. But it's not to be ruled out. There may have been somebody else, acting independently of Redwine and his friends, who couldn't afford to have the first body identified—but who didn't mind about Redwine's body a bit. The vehicle that's been brought to the foot of this crag may have belonged to that other person—or party."

"Party?"

"The dead man—the first dead man—may not have been wholly unsupported. He may have felt it wise to have friends lurking round too. Think of that column of smoke. It may have been a signal."

David considered. "Can't we go further?" he asked. "Can't we now say it couldn't have been anything else? My first notion that somebody was cooking a chop, or boiling a kettle, just doesn't hold water."

"And the kettle doesn't, either. For there wasn't a kettle. Except what you might call a pretty kettle of fish." Appleby smiled. "And there was certainly that. I mean there was certainly the devil of a crisis for somebody. But there's another possibility about that fire, you know. It seems, from your account, to have been quite a small-scale affair. It might have been a matter of the burning of a few papers. . . . No, don't go up there, Henchman."

David had been pacing about—without much noticing the fact, for his brain was racing. And he had been just about to climb to the rim of rock that faced the Loaf. Now he stopped, and stared at Appleby. "You think—?"

"The sky-line mayn't be entirely healthy at the moment." Appleby dropped this casually. "Now, what was I saying?"

David took a long breath. "Something about burning papers."

"Precisely. Your man—the first man—may have felt himself trapped up here with a batch of papers he was determined shouldn't fall into enemy hands. So he may have put a match to them."

"Not a signal after all!"

Appleby got off his shooting stick. "In point of pure theory," he said, "that doesn't follow."

"I'm afraid I don't understand."

"Detective investigation, like philosophy in the University of Oxford, has its empyrean, its speculative inane. Scramble up to that empyrean in the present case, Henchman, and you have to admit that your friend may have been killing two birds with one stone. He may have been destroying something. And he may have been making a signal as well."

"Then he was damned clever, if you ask me." David had experienced one of his quick spurts of impatience.

"Quite so. And there's no lack of cleverness, I assure you, among the sort of people you and I are involved with at the moment."

"It doesn't seem to prevent their getting killed."

"Very true. But I suspect the cleverest of them are alive still—and ready to give a kick when they get the chance."

"And you and I are going to try conclusions with them?" David had moved to the farther side of the summit, and was peering with due caution into the late afternoon. "You've certainly cleared a ring for the job."

"Cleared a ring? I'm afraid not." Appleby was amused. "One doesn't, I assure you, conduct affairs of this sort upon romantic principles. Far from it." He looked at his watch. "It would be an exaggeration to say that this moor's now an armed camp. But it's no longer as unfrequented as it looks."

David didn't know whether to feel relieved or let down. "They must know," he said. "Presumably they don't think in romantic terms either. They must guess that you and I aren't, after all, out on an utterly exposed limb."

Appleby nodded soberly. "That's no doubt true. But they may feel they have a good deal at stake. At least your friend in the knickerbockers may feel that. And his nondescript assistant. Presumably you could identify either of them."

"I don't know about the assistant. I haven't much of a picture of him. But I'd certainly know the chap in knickerbockers. I had one long straight look at him—or rather two —at the pineapple nectar place. I'm a liability during the rest of his days, all right—just as I would have been with Redwine." David paused. "I suppose that means that I really am in some sort of hazard until—well, we get him. I doubt whether the nondescript assistant's up to much. He lacked guts, I thought. But the knickerbocker chap— who seems the only other person under any threat from me—would take a stiff risk, I agree."

"Quite so. And when you vanished at the Point to Point he'd turn his thoughts back to Knack Tor at once. He'd know you'd be brought back—by the police. And he'd know that he himself would be, so to speak, an expected guest. But I think he'd feel it was a wonderful chance, all the same. Particularly with night coming along."

David grinned. "Which is why we've had this leisurely chat?"

"Just that. And I'd expect him to be on location by now.

119

How would you approach the matter, if you were in his shoes?"

"I'd do one of two things. Either I'd take the line masked by the Loaf—and be on the Loaf now. Or I'd think that too obvious and risky, and tackle the very ticklish business of finding and gaining cover on our own likely line of retreat."

Appleby nodded. "I think you're right. And it rather depends on what he feels he can do with that rifle. . . . He never really had a chance of a fair pot at you?"

"Not until the pineapple nectar place. And then he felt it was too risky."

Appleby disengaged his shooting-stick from its cranny in the rock. "It's just possible that he may be a crack shot —which is a very different thing from being a thoroughly good one. . . . And now, we've got a spot of work."

"Work?"

"We've got to locate him, if we can. Take your clothes off."

David stared. "What did you say?"

"I asked you to take your clothes off. Sweater and shorts."

Considerably to his own surprise, David found himself obeying this strange injunction. He wriggled out of his khaki pants and sky-blue wind-cheater without a notion of what his action was in aid of. It was only when he saw Appleby stripping himself of his own tweeds that a suspicion of the truth dawned on him. "Look here," he said, "you can't possibly do that! I can't allow it!"

He was too late. Appleby's head was already in the wind-cheater. And when he had pulled it down over himself, and scrambled into the shorts, he turned to David for a moment with a look that was wholly formidable. "Be quiet, Henchman. This is a purely professional phase in

120

the affair. You can't be of the slightest help to me."

"You must stop!" David was amazingly angry. "I won't let you . . . you ought to have explained . . . it's quite unfair!" He took a step forward and made a grab at Appleby. But Appleby simply feinted like a deft three-quarter, jumped over Redwine's body, and in a flash was scrambling up to the rim of their rocky platform on the side facing the Loaf. And there he stood, gazing out over the moor.

A chill wind was now blowing stiffly. Even in the shallow cup of the summit it made itself felt, whipping round David's bare thighs. Up above, it caught at Appleby's iron-grey hair and blew it about his forehead. But his figure was as slim as David's own. So the deception—

Suddenly Appleby bent at the knees, tumbled to the rock, rolled over, and came down in a crumpled heap at David's feet. And in the same instant David heard a sharp crack. He knew instantly that it was no tin-pot pistol this time. The rifle had really been brought into operation at last.

"Well—we've located him, all right."

David felt his inside turn queerly over. It just hadn't occurred to him—in the split second that had passed—that Appleby wasn't dead. But of course he wasn't—although he sounded pretty shaken by his fall. Nobody could bring off a shot like that from the Loaf. Or not in a wind.

Appleby had scrambled to his feet and was skinning off the wind-cheater once more. "It's rather nice," he said cheerfully. "But I must let you have it back, all the same."

David found himself giving a long gasp. His eyes were fixed not on Appleby but on a rock a couple of yards from his feet. He took a step forward, stooped, and picked up something that lay there. "Did you feel it a close

121

thing?" he asked.

Appleby shook his head. "Dear me, no. It was silly of him to give away his position for the sake of so very slim a chance. In a wind, you know—"

"I was thinking that myself. But I was wrong." David held out his closed hand, and then slowly opened it. It held a lock of iron-grey hair. "If you run to a personal museum," he said gravely, "you may care to add this to it." And suddenly he was furious again. "I'll never forgive you," he said. "Never!"

16 "IF IT'S TO be an affair of honour, we can fix up a duel later on." Appleby had got himself into his decorous elderly trousers. "What are you called by your intimates?"

David glowered at him. "David."

"Well, I think I now qualify. So look sharp, David, and prepare to join the hunt. I'd hate to keep you out of that." He gave the quick faint smile that had first persuaded David he was all right. "Perhaps you'll be in at the kill, and forgive me after all."

David hauled up his shorts, and continued to scowl. "What do you mean—the hunt?" he asked ungraciously.

"The forces of the law should now be closing in on the Loaf. We'll climb up and have a look. But remember your army training, David. That rifle's still in commission, remember. And your knickerbockered friend must be one of the best shots in England."

Cautiously they clambered to the rim of rock again and peered over. The Loaf seemed absurdly far away. And there was no movement anywhere. "Isn't it a complication?" By asking this question, David was acknowledging that he had resumed diplomatic relations with Appleby. "I mean, his being a crack shot?"

"It certainly is. And it partly explains the big risk he's

123

taken in the effort to get you—as he now probably believes he's done. He reckons he can shoot himself out of any hasty trap we've constructed. What my local colleagues will have assembled is a dozen armed police. They'll have heard the shot, and be spreading out on the other side of the Loaf now. They can bring up a good many more, if necessary, quite soon. And eventually, of course, we could have troops."

"It would be a sort of siege."

"Yes—and rather a cautious one. There would be no point in risking lives."

"I suppose not." David remembered Appleby in his wind-cheater. "But isn't the chap more likely to make a break for it?"

"He certainly is—in which case he must just be trailed until he's exhausted." Appleby had got out his binoculars and was scanning the Loaf. "We may have an all-night show. There's a moon."

For David, lying beside Appleby on the rock, these words were oddly evocative. Perhaps it was because he had himself had a moonlight adventure of sorts the night before. Pictures began forming themselves in his head of extraordinary incidents to come. In order to discourage himself from this woolgathering, he came rather hastily out with something. "I've had an idea," he said.

"That's always useful." Appleby didn't lower his binoculars. But his tone was encouraging.

"It's about my man—the first man to be shot. He wasn't shot up here at all—not, I mean, on the spot and with the little pistol. He was shot at long range from the Loaf, just as you nearly were a few minutes ago."

"But you say there was a pistol lying beside him—or actually in his hand—when you found him."

"Yes, I know. But Redwine had just climbed up and

planted that, in order to make the thing look like suicide."
David now spoke rapidly, for his theory was opening
out before him. "You see, Redwine and the man in knickerbockers couldn't get up here to tackle the chap, because
the chap was himself armed. But they picked him off from
the Loaf, and then Redwine came up and—as I say—
planted the pistol, while at the same time pocketing the
chap's own gun—the gun he'd been holding them at bay
with."

"I think I can see some of our people coming now."
Appleby was sweeping the horizon beyond the Loaf. "And
presumably there will be some behind us, on the track
where we've left the car." He slipped the binocular-strap
over his head and handed the instrument to David. "Get
over to the other side and have a look."

David took the binoculars. "You don't think much of my
theory?"

"Well, you know, if you plant a rifle-bullet in a man's
head from a distance, you can scarcely hope to get away
with the proposition that he's shot himself with a small
pistol."

"Of course not—if and when the body's properly examined. But this body promptly disappeared."

Appleby nodded. "So it did—to be replaced by another
one, certainly shot at close range, and pretty certainly by
the revolver we see lying there. Your theory's a good start,
if I may say so, in criminal investigation, but it would be
better if it gave any hint why one body has been replaced
by another. That's the crux of the matter, as it seems to
me. . . . Now, can you see anybody on that track?"

"I can see your car—just." David was still focussing the
binoculars. "And—by jove!—I can see two more. They're
just driving up."

"Ah—my local colleagues are out in force." Appleby

125

was pleased. "It's just as well. Our friend on the Loaf needs taking seriously, as we've seen."

"They're getting out. I say!"—David was suddenly alarmed—"they'll know he's got a rifle. But will they know he's such a deadly shot?"

Appleby was folding his shooting stick. "They certainly won't."

"And will these police who have just arrived beside your car even know that he's on the Loaf?"

"It depends whether they've brought walkie-talkie stuff and are in communication with the police on the other side. But you'll tell them, David, anyway."

"I'll tell them?" David was surprised.

"Precisely. That's your job. You get down from the summit here on the far side, just where you originally came up. I think you can get over the rim without being commanded from the Loaf, but you'd better make that part of the operation as nippy as you can. Then you make for those chaps who've just arrived by the track—but on a detour that keeps Knack Tor between you and the Loaf until you're entirely out of range, which you'd better regard as at another two hundred yards. And then you report on the situation to whoever you find in charge."

"I see. But I don't know that I call that joining the hunt."

"Then you can call it an order instead. But I think you'll find there's plenty excitement to come."

"What about you?" David turned round and looked at Appleby.

"I'll stick here for a few minutes until you're well off the map. Then I'll go down the same way myself and work right round the Loaf, so as to meet the police coming up on it from the other side. They must have their warning, too."

"I suppose they must. But how are you going to find cover?"

"Oh, there'll be cover all right." Appleby spoke briskly. "We've been rather exaggerating the nakedness of this moor."

"I see. Well, why shouldn't it be me who goes in that direction?"

"You must just regard it as another order." Appleby was good-humoured. "And I think, perhaps, I'd better have the glasses again. But just take another look at the police coming from the track, and see if you can count them."

David did as he was told. It wasn't easy to get a clear view, because he had to focus almost straight into a sun now low in the west. He was silent for a moment, and then asked a question. "Will they be the sort of police that wear helmets, or flat peaked caps?"

Appleby was puzzled. "Caps, I think. But can't you make them out?"

"They don't seem to be wearing anything at all—on their heads, I mean. In fact"—he hesitated—". . . I don't think they are policemen. I'm sure they're not . . . Oh, I say!"

Appleby glanced across at him. "My dear man," he asked, "what's taken you?"

"The cars—drawn up behind yours. I recognise them. The front one's the Heap."

"The what?"

"It's our name for Timothy's tourer. And the other is Pettifor's own, a Land Rover. It's not the police. It's them." And David laughed rather unsteadily. "It's my reading-party—Pettifor's lot."

The amusement with which Appleby received this strange intelligence struck David as a trifle forced. He had

127

been expecting police. And when somebody important at Scotland Yard expects police it is only once in a blue moon, presumably, that police don't turn up. To be offered a gaggle of undergraduates instead was a situation requiring the exercise of some self-control. And this must hold particularly of such a development when it occurred in the vicinity of a murderously inclined sharpshooter of exceptional skill. David was wondering whether it was up to him to apologise for this remarkable intrusion when Appleby spoke first.

"At least it's policemen on the other side of the Loaf. I've glimpsed a couple of them with the naked eye. And they're lying pretty low, I'm glad to say—just as our friend is, up there with the rifle. How many of your companions are advancing upon us?"

"I'm trying to count. I can see Ogg. He's got a beard. I think they're all there. Except Ian Dancer."

"It would be too much to expect him. And your tutor?"

"Yes, Pettifor's there."

"You fill me with curiosity, David. But I think I'd better not come across and look. I fancied I saw a hint of movement on the Loaf. Is there anybody else?"

"Yes, there's the affluent retired clergyman—a chap called Faircloth. And Colonel Farquharson, a melancholic admirer of the young manhood of England." The irruption of the reading-party had momentarily thrown David into one of his light-headed fits, and he was disposed to talk any nonsense that occurred to him. "Large-limbed Off —who's in Milton, you know—is in the van. Or am I imagining the whole damned thing?"

"Do you suppose your companions have missed you, and that this is in the nature of a rescue party?"

"Good lord, no!" This extravagant suggestion turned David sober again. "Nobody would care twopence if I

didn't turn up till midnight. This is just one of the archae-
ologising jaunts that sometimes get themselves organised
in the afternoon. That's why Dr. Faircloth's there. He goes
in for hut circles and burial chambers and things. He's
gesturing and pointing now. Come to think of it, he was
burbling about Knack Tor this morning."

"I see. Well, cut down and tell them all to clear out."

"To clear out?" David was surprised and even mildly
offended by the brusqueness of this.

"Certainly." Appleby's tone was suddenly impatient.
"Unless they want burial chambers laid on all round.
What's the fellow up there going to make of a mob like
that? Are they in a bunch?"

"Yes—they're in a bunch, all right."

"He'll take them for a hunt—a hunt of talented ama-
teurs like yourself. And if something snaps in him—as is
always a possibility with a fellow like this in a crisis—
he'll shoot his way through them as soon as sneeze. Your
friends would be more safely employed playing chicken,
any day. So go and take them out of it."

"Don't be absurd, sir." David had never felt more in-
subordinate in his life. "They're a perfectly able-bodied
crowd."

"They've all got bodies perfectly able to stop a bullet.
Go down and take them back to their cars, please. They
needn't go farther than that. There simply must be a few
armed police coming along that track any time now."

David felt there was nothing for it but to obey. He went
across to Appleby, handed over the binoculars without a
word, returned to the other side of the summit and lowered himself over the edge. He hadn't gone down this way
before—although it was the way he had first come up—
and for some seconds he thought he wasn't going to manage it at all. Perhaps the tea and sandwiches hadn't quite

129

got him back to par, or perhaps it was particularly tricky downward going anyway. He had lowered himself only a few feet when he got stuck—spread-eagled against the rock, and seemingly with nothing practicable that he could lower either hand to. Of course there must be something, since his toes had somewhere found a hold where his chest now was. He squinted sideways down; the foot of the rockface seemed suddenly very far away—and then slowly what he could glimpse of it began to sway and circle. That was what they called vertigo. He shut his eyes and remained very still. And in this immobile moment he heard a single sharp exclamation above him. It was Appleby's voice. Appleby had sworn aloud.

And somehow David didn't like that. He had a notion that this admirably controlled person wasn't much given to facile oaths. "Is anything up?" he shouted.

"If you can put on a bit of speed, do." Appleby's voice was quite calm. "He's moving. But I'd better not move myself until I see him taking a line."

"Right oh, sir."

"And David . . . can you hear me still?"

"Yes, perfectly."

"Tell them, if you like, about there being a body up here—and with a bullet in it. They'd better understand the situation's serious. But keep mum on Redwine's name, and on any talk of spy-stuff. That's confidential between you and me, and it's possible I may want to sit on his identity for a bit. Got that?"

"I've got it." David discovered that during this exchange he had come all right again. His giddiness had vanished so suddenly and so entirely that he could hardly believe it had attacked him. His hands had found their hold, and first one then the other toe were competently at work. In a few moments he was at the foot of the rock, standing on turf. And he ran. It was like old times.

He wondered what on earth he was going to say. From down here Pettifor and company weren't at the moment visible, but he knew just what direction he must take to meet them head on. In what brief but convincing formula was he going to give old Pettifor orders for a right-about-turn? How was he going to stem the amiable and loquacious Faircloth's enquiries about his progress through the *Republic* of Plato? And what would Timothy Dumble make of him, thus careering over the moor with urgent injunctions to flee from dangers unknown? His representations simply wouldn't make sense. And he remembered, with a sudden sinking heart, that his last appearance among his companions had been as the man who grabbed the wheel of Timothy's car. Reason told him that that had been all right and that they knew it; that they had thought more of him at the end of that imbecile game of chicken than they had at the beginning. But something else inside him made him feel—to put it mildly—the full awkwardness of taking on once more the role of the prudent man; and of taking it on, this time, amid circumstances of the largest melodrama.

However, David continued to run. He had accepted his mission from Appleby, who was the professional in charge of the affair, and he must push it through, even if there was no comfort in it. He didn't reflect—perhaps because he was running too hard for much reflection—that on the barest reckoning he had quite a lot to show in the way of honourable scars and war-paint. A bullet in the heel of a shoe, a grazed finger, the familiar acquaintance of a certain Sir John Appleby who knew all about top-ranking spies: it would all have added up if he'd had leisure to think of it. But his business was running over this moor; and fortunately it was something at which he possessed a modest expertness now. The boggy bits, the patches with thick bracken, the places where the tumps of turf disappeared entirely amid a proliferation of heath or heather; he knew how to look out for these and by-pass them with an economical detour. If this awkward job had to be done, he could at least be sure of doing it tolerably well.

Not that his speed was first class; he was too near the end of a long day for that. And the light was no longer too good. For shooting—he thought grimly—it would still be tip-top; but in a small-scale way the ground was mottled with deep shadows which made tricky the business of placing one's flying feet. This required nearly all his concentration. Yet he did manage to think about what was the likely situation behind him. Appleby's exclamation had suggested some critical turn in the affair; and that must mean that the movement of the man in knickerbockers— if indeed he was the marksman—was in the direction of the track and of Pettifor's party. He would have become aware of the police cautiously advancing on the other side of the Loaf, and he would be intent on making his escape this way. In fact he was probably somewhere on the moor behind David now. And there couldn't be much doubt that he'd have his rifle with him still.

David had just arrived at this conclusion when he breasted a swell of the moor and found that he had reached his goal. Here they were. Or at least here, well ahead of the others, was the infant Ogg.

17 "HULLO, DAVID—WE didn't expect to find you here." As Ogg shouted this, he gave a wave with one hand and an encouraging tug at his beard with the other.

"Are they all following you?" David was breathless.

"Yes. But I came ahead. The expedition doesn't seem a great success. Old Pettifor's gloomy. Faircloth won't stop talking, and I think that gets on his nerves. And Farquharson's come, too, although we didn't really ask him. He's awfully odd. I don't understand him at all. Is that Knack Tor? The idea is that we're to get to the top of it."

"Well, you won't." Planting himself in Ogg's path, David spoke abruptly. "You're all to clear out."

"To clear out!" Ogg, not unnaturally, was indignant at this brusque instruction. "Whatever do you mean?"

"I mean, for one thing, that there's a corpse up there—with a bullet through its head."

"Honour bright?" Ogg's eyes rounded. "But how horrible. I must see that. I'm going up."

"You're doing nothing of the sort, my boy; it's not for general exhibition. There's a high-up copper who says so. So right-about-turn."

This implied reflection on Ogg's tender years was scarcely tactful, and it didn't go down well. He could be seen to flush above—and indeed through—his beard. But now the rest of the reading-party was coming up, and Ogg turned and shouted at them. "I say, here's David—and he's more badly cracked than ever! He says we can't go on. Come and get him under control, you chaps."

At this, numerous cries at once broke out. It did seem as if the expedition had been in rather a gloomy way, and as if its younger members were inclined to jump at any diversion.

"Can't go on? Poor old David! Sunstroke, I expect. Thinks he's Horatius guarding the bridge."

"Or the Leech Gatherer, with an enormous amount to say."

"David believes he's the Solitary."

"David's convinced he's the Female Vagrant."

"Resolution and Independence."

"Behold him single in the field."

"Him whom we love, our idiot boy . . . good old David!"

This was quite as bad as anything David had expected. It wasn't possible to be offended, because each of the silly asses was grinning at him more affectionately than the others. As for Dr. Faircloth, he positively beamed. It was evident that this orgy of Wordsworthian banter appealed to his cultivated mind. David raised both hands. "Shut up!" he shouted.

And they actually shut up—perhaps more because of his look than of his voice. In the resulting silence he thought he heard men calling to each other, somewhere far behind him. It must be the police.

At this moment Pettifor came up. He and the melancholy Colonel Farquharson had been trailing behind the rest of the party. "Hullo, David," he said. "What's this?"

"It's . . . it's a· sort of police matter, sir." Pettifor at least was sensible, but David found it difficult to get launched on his facts. "The police are trying to round up a chap who's got loose with a rifle, and they want us all out of the way."

"That's not what he told me at all!" Ogg broke in eagerly. "He was babbling about a corpse on the top of the Tor. I tell you, he's gone right round the bend."

David did his best to be patient. "There is that, too—a dead man up there. He's been shot. And there's a police-man—an important one from Scotland Yard. His name's Appleby."

"Appleby! Not Sir John Appleby?"

This—sharply and unexpectedly—had come from Far-quharson. David nodded. "That's right. Do you know him?"

"Certainly. He's an Assistant Commissioner of the Met-ropolitan Police, or some such nonsense. So you're right to call him important, no doubt. But I can't see why he should be up there with a corpse."

"It's a long story." David could hear shouting more distinctly now, and he felt rather desperate. "The point is, he wants us to go back as far as the cars. His is the big car you must have seen. There should be other police pull-ing up there any time, in order to try and cut this chap off. It's a matter of guns and things, and I was told to bring a message that we must all go back."

"Then back we'd better go." Timothy Dumble, who had been listening silently to all this, spoke with decision. "David's been in on this, and he gives the orders, if you ask me. Don't you agree, sir?"

Pettifor, thus appealed to in what were not particularly pupillary tones, nodded acquiescence. It was always re-garded as a point in his favour that, upon appropriate oc-casions, he did what he was told. "No doubt you are right," he said. "And it's not for an elderly civilian to demur. Faircloth, what do you say?"

Faircloth—very inappositely, as it seemed to David— produced his comfortable laugh. "Certainly, certainly. But I strongly suspect that we are having our legs pulled. Yes —our young friends are diverting themselves, if you ask me."

"But it all appears most circumstantial." Pettifor, leaning back on his walking-stick, seemed prepared to talk at entire leisure. "For instance, David mentions a certain Sir John Appleby; and with Farquharson this Appleby's name and calling at once, as they say, ring a bell. You haven't heard of this Appleby yourself?"

Faircloth didn't answer this. Instead, he cocked up his benign head and listened. "Do you know," he said, "I think I hear something that really might be called a hue and cry? How very remarkable!" His voice admitted a touch of alarm. "It will no doubt be wise that we withdraw as we are advised."

And then Leon Kryder spoke. He too had been listening for distant sounds. "I don't know about this Appleby ringing a bell," he said. "But I guess he's blowing a whistle right now."

There could be no doubt about the whistle. And it made David shiver—for he was reminded of the bad moment that morning when Redwine had, with a similar summons, conjured his assistant out of the moor. Well, Redwine would never blow a whistle again. And this time it was certainly the police; one blast was answering another, and there were shouts among which he thought that Appleby's voice could be distinguished. It seemed likely that the hunt was coming this way, and that he hadn't managed to get these chattering people away in time, after all.

136

The next moment, the truth of this conjecture was apparent to him. With surprising suddenness, the man in knickerbockers had appeared not a hundred yards off. He must have found a line of cover that masked the first part of his retreat from the Loaf. Perhaps he had accomplished it crawling, or on all fours. But he was on his feet and running now. And his rifle was in his hands.

Arthur Drury, the quiet man who didn't get on with Timothy, had seen the fugitive, too. He turned to David. "Is that the chap?" he asked. "He's got a queer notion of making a bolt for it, if he is."

This was true. The man in knickerbockers was zigzagging across the open moor as if it were a rugger field with a dozen players to weave through if he was to score a try. For a moment David supposed that this strange course really did represent some sort of calculated evasive action, as when a ship tacks about when under threat of assault by torpedoes. Then he saw that there could be no sense in that. Even if the man had been brought under fire by the police—which was unlikely, since he didn't seem to be giving battle—there could be no advantage in such a technique.

"He's been hit on the head, if you ask me," Arthur Drury went on. "And he's in a bit of a daze. I don't see why we shouldn't collar him."

"That's not David's orders." Timothy produced this opposition promptly. "So back we go." He turned to Pettifor. "Isn't that the drill, sir?"

"Quite right. Stand not upon the order of your going, but go at once." Pettifor had a trick of these silly tags and quotations that would never desert him in any exigency. He seemed quite unconscious of them and always brought them out as if they had never been uttered before. And now he showed no sign of budging himself. He had un-

137

cased his ancient field-glasses and was focussing them. "Dear me!" he exclaimed, "the fellow's covered with blood."

"Blood-bolter'd Banquo," Ogg thought it enormously amusing to echo this habit of his uncle's.

Tom Overend spoke for the first time. He was usually rational, and David had some hope of him. "Total gules," Tom said.

David despaired of them. The man in knickerbockers had now taken a tack that was bringing him at them head on. And he was certainly a bloody sight. Perhaps there really had been a gun-battle farther back, and one of the police had put a bullet in him. Or perhaps he had been shot at as a justifiable preventive measure. Only David hadn't heard a single report.

"Taken a tumble," Timothy said. "Was he up Knack Tor?"

David shook his head. "The Loaf." Timothy, he felt, had got it right. In beginning his get-away the man in knicker-bockers must have come down with a crack, and he was in some badly confused state. This certainly didn't make him any less dangerous—quite the contrary. And now he had spotted them. He had spotted the mild archaeological field-party: three elderly men and a gaggle of talkative youths. He was coming unsteadily to a halt. And he was raising his rifle.

"Get down! Get down, all of you!" It was Farquharson who gave this yell—and as he uttered it he pitched himself with unexpected agility at Ogg's knees. A damned good mark for him, David thought.

There was a sharp crack. The man had opened fire. David found that his own nose was buried in heather. There was no longer the slightest hope of safety in retreat. He flattened himself on the earth and simply hoped that everybody else had done the same. Not that there was much help in that, either. If the man in knickerbockers was seeing red, he could produce a holocaust. David waited for a fusillade. But it didn't happen. Nothing made itself heard except shouts. They were coming nearer. But they were a good long way off, all the same. He put his head up cautiously. The man in knickerbockers was running again, and had left them on his flank. His course was straighter now. He was making for the track and the cars.

"Gone away!"

It was Ogg's shout, and it brought David to his feet with an instant sense of fresh crisis. The others were getting up, too, and he saw a circle of startled faces around him, mostly attached to bodies still on all-fours. The effect was of a small perturbed herd of unlikely ruminants, and he would have laughed aloud if he hadn't at once been appalled by a realisation of what the new disaster was. The incredible Ogg was fifty yards away, and hotfoot after the man in knickerbockers. He was advertising himself as he ran by cries borrowed from the hunting field. "Gone away!" Ogg yelled again. "Tally-ho, chaps, tally-ho!" He had been vastly affronted, David guessed, by the indignity, as he conceived it, of Farquharson's timely tackle, and now he was showing that he was a man to be taken seriously. David remembered the infant's excitement the night before. This was the same thing; it was valley-of-death stuff again.

And Pettifor's lot, of course, responded as they must. They scrambled to their feet, cursed Ogg roundly, and went tearing after him. David found to his fury that he couldn't quite keep up with any of them. His effective running was over for that day. But no more could the others keep up with Ogg. Their large-limbed infant had an incredible turn of speed. It was his line, David remembered;

139

he had been some sort of stripling champion; and this strong card had clearly made him the readier to take his present utterly rash action. He was overtaking the man in knickerbockers hand over fist.

It looked, David thought, thoroughly ugly. The police, indeed, had now appeared. Glancing over his shoulder, he could see several of them up with Pettifor, Faircloth and Farquharson already. But they didn't look like getting very effectively into the picture, all the same—or not unless a fresh bunch of them made their overdue appearance on the track ahead.

The man in knickerbockers was nearing the track now. And David realised that he had a plan. If he had brought any transport of his own it must have been somewhere on the farther side of the moor, so that he was now cut off from it. He was going to take his chance of getting away in one of the empty cars waiting straight in front of him. It looked as if Ogg had some prospect of overtaking him as he ran, or at least of coming up with him as he was trying to start one car or another. And if Ogg managed that, the unfortunate youth's chances of survival were slim.

The others were trying to stop Ogg by shouting. But either he took their cries for encouragement, or he was determined to pay no attention to them. And the man in knickerbockers knew how closely he was being pursued; David had seen him give a glance over his shoulder and take the situation in. At any moment he might pause, turn, and simply pick Ogg off. Unless he was pretty well blinded by his own blood—and certainly, at close range, he had looked bloody enough—there was no chance of his failing to bring off such a shot.

But now there was a new factor in the situation. Appleby had appeared as if from nowhere and was coming up on the flank of the crazy pursuit. He must quickly have

140

followed David down from the summit of the Tor and taken his own rapid route towards the track. He still had his shooting-stick; he still had his pork-pie hat; doubtless he still had his little cardboard label. He hadn't anything like Ogg's speed, but he looked as if he could hold his own with the man in knickerbockers. But that didn't look quite good enough. The man was now on the track, and making for Timothy's car. Ogg wasn't fifty yards behind him. David prayed that Timothy had left the ignition-key in the Heap, and that the wretched old contraption would start like a bird. It would mean the man's getting away. But it would mean that Ogg wouldn't provide this beastly day's third corpse.

There was a wrathful shout from immediately ahead. It was Timothy; even in this grim situation he had an additional indignant bellow for the spectacle of somebody actually proposing to liberate his car. And the man in knickerbockers had, in fact, now jumped into it. He was pitching his rifle down on the front seat and furiously attacking the controls. And nothing happened.

Nothing was happening. David knew that even at this distance one would decidedly hear the sound the Heap made when it started into life. And Ogg was making straight for it; he wasn't a stone's throw away; either he was completely crazy or the world's most courageous infant. The man in knickerbockers was keeping an eye on him; he straightened up, seized the rifle and took aim. If he outed Ogg—and then Appleby—he would have a couple of minutes in hand. Appleby was still running. He had raised his shooting-stick—rather as if trying to hail an elusive taxi, so that for a second there was the effect of a grotesque, a macabre farce. Then the rifle seemed to spin itself out of the hands of the man in knickerbockers and vanish. There was a faint report, and from Ogg a faint triumphant shout. But the man wasn't giving in. He had sat down again at the wheel—and suddenly there was a roar and a clatter as the engine fired. He flung it into gear and the car went off with a jerk. Ogg, sprinting up, just failed to make a successful grab at the hood. The man in knickerbockers was making his escape. But Ogg remained alive.

And he remained resourceful as well. He ran on, and within seconds had hurled himself into Pettifor's Land Rover. He had it started in a flash. With a fantastic effect of unreality—of the unashamedly cinematographic—the pursuit and flight were continuing. In a whirl of dust the two cars disappeared down the track.

The group of pursuers ahead had halted. There was nothing more to do. David ran on and joined them. And Timothy turned to him, panting. "What frightful cheek! But I'm glad it's not the other way on."

"The other way on?"

"Not the brat that's in the Heap. It's temperamental to-day. The steering. I think it was one of those pot-holes last night."

"We'll see them again in a second." Arthur Drury was pointing. "There, by the next rise. If the frightful old thing lasts that far."

"What d'you mean—lasts that far?" With some inconsistency, Timothy was at once indignant.

"There they go!" Tom Overend gave a shout.

"Sure—there they go!" And Leon Kryder pointed. "Gone away and tally-ho!"

They were all wildly excited. But David didn't feel that way at all. He supposed he'd had enough. As he watched the two cars shoot into view again in the middle distance he felt that interest had drained out of him. He didn't want Ogg to come to any grief, but otherwise he couldn't

142

care less. . . . And then suddenly he found that his nerves were tingling, and that his eyes were glued in fascination on the leading car. It was going at a great pace—and it was swaying queerly. The movement lasted only for a fraction of a second, but it was entirely horrible. And so was what instantly followed. The Heap spun strangely round on its own tail, rolled over and over and vanished.

Everybody gasped and began to run. A few seconds later, they gasped again. Ogg had brought the Land Rover safely to a halt. But close by where the other car had hurtled from the track there was black smoke and leaping flame.

The Heap, when they got to it, was a smouldering mess. Ogg, very quiet and pale, was sitting on the grass, seemingly unable to take his eyes from the thing that he and Appleby had hauled from the fire. His hands would need attending to. But he wasn't hurt.

"Did you recognise him, too?" Presently David managed to ask Appleby this in a tolerably steady way. What had been the man in knickerbockers didn't look at all nice. But the body didn't in the least approximate to a cinder.

Appleby shook his head. "I never saw him before."

"Do you think it was the steering, or the crack he got when he began to bolt?"

"Perhaps a bit of both. Anyway, he's dead. So our very restricted cast has grown smaller still."

"I think it's awful. I suppose I should be relieved, since there can't be anyone left who wants to come after me with a gun." David managed to smile wanly. He felt he wanted to get away from everybody and go to bed. "But I just feel it's all awful."

"Is it? It's certainly all very mysterious still. Which is unsatisfactory, you know. There's quite a lot to be done."

David contrived to brace himself. "All right. Straight away, if you like."

Appleby smiled. "Good. But I think, as a matter of fact, we can conveniently ring down the curtain for a bit of an interval. Unless there's something you want to go at immediately yourself."

And suddenly David remembered. "Yes, please," he said. "It's about how the chap lost his rifle when he was just going to shoot Ogg. How did it happen?"

Appleby looked surprised. "I managed to shoot it out of his hands."

"To shoot it!" David stared—and then his glance went to the ground beside Appleby. "You mean to say—?"

"Precisely." And Appleby picked up his shooting-stick. "Doesn't it seem reasonable that a shooting-stick should shoot?"

"I suppose so." David was so astonished that he offered this reply in entire seriousness. And then he grinned. "Is it a standard issue to high-ups at Scotland Yard?"

"Dear me, no. It's private enterprise—and I've no doubt unique in England. As a matter of fact, it was invented for me by my eldest boy." And Appleby glanced round Pettifor's lot. "A quiet, serious lad. We've sent him to Cambridge, as a matter of fact."

ii *JOHN APPLEBY*

APPLEBY DROVE INTO Nymph Monachorum
after dinner. Presumably the reading-party
had by this time recruited itself after the
hazards of the day, and some members of
it at least could stand up to a little questioning. Appleby's
own meal had been hasty; there had been, not unnaturally,
various local authorities to see; and there had also been
certain crucial telephone enquiries to make in London.
When he got to the George he asked for Pettifor.

And Pettifor appeared at once and led him into a deserted smoking-room. "I hope you don't want young David
Henchman," he said. "The boy's tired out. He lacks the
season of all natures, sleep. I've packed him off to bed."

"Quite right." If Appleby thought this manner of speech
mildly strange, he said nothing. "And you must understand, Mr. Pettifor, that I have no official concern with
this affair. But as I got mixed up in it, I think I ought to
try and see it through. I think you know the Chief Constable down here?"

"Dear me, yes. We're distantly related." Pettifor smiled.
"This is my part of the world, you see—and we're all in
some sort of relationship with each other."

"No doubt. Well, I was only going to say that I've been
in touch with him, and he quite agrees to my looking into

147

this affair. As for Henchman, I've no desire to rout him out of bed. But I'd like a word with you about him. This has been a bad business, and he's been right in the thick of it."

"If there's anything I can properly tell you, Sir John, I shall, of course, do so." Pettifor's tone was slightly chilly. Appleby, he seemed to be saying, was only a policeman, after all. And one doesn't much chat to policemen about one's pupils.

"Thank you very much." Appleby was unperturbed. "He tells an extraordinary story. But I can say at once that I see no reason to doubt his good faith. What he may have missed, or what he may have muddled, is of course another matter."

Pettifor shook his head. "I think he'd miss or muddle very little. I regard him as a thoroughly reliable man. And discreet. Would I be right, Sir John, in thinking that he possesses information which you have asked him not to spread?"

"You would be quite right." Appleby, although rather startled, answered readily.

"I somehow formed the impression that he knew the identity of this man who was killed on Knack Tor. But he would not discuss the matter. On such occasions, David's lips are locked."

Appleby said nothing. But he looked steadily at Pettifor, for he had an obscure feeling that he had heard something distinctly odd. And the man looked odd—or at least he looked oddly done up. He had, of course, learned that one of the young men in his charge had spent the better part of the day being hunted for his life. And he had seen with his own eyes another of them—who was incidentally his own nephew—in the most imminent risk of being shot dead. These facts were no doubt sufficient to account for

148

an impression of strain or exhaustion in him. But there was something else. Appleby wondered if it was some sort of fanaticism. Elderly dons were sometimes like that. They spent their time dishing out such a lot of intellectual and personal tolerance that they went mildly mad on this specific topic or that, and would be utterly intransigent over it. Perhaps Pettifor had a hobby-horse of that sort. But it was hard to see how it could tie up with the mystery. "About Henchman," Appleby asked. "Do you know whether he has any acquaintance or relations round about here?"

"I am almost certain he has none. None of the men has, except Dancer—Ian Dancer. He wasn't with us on our expedition. He has relations with whom he sometimes stays for the hunting. And, as a matter of fact, he had a riding accident this afternoon, and got back to the George only half-an-hour ago. His story is rather obscure, but I gather he required some medical attention. He's gone to bed too."

Appleby nodded. "I know about Dancer. I ought to mention that I'm staying for a few days with my wife's people at Dream."

"Indeed." Pettifor took crisp note of this social fact. "Of course my nephew, Julian Ogg, is also acquainted with people round about—if the matter has any significance for you."

"Your nephew displayed, if I may say so, remarkable courage." Appleby offered this comment in the way of tact, for Pettifor's tone had been slightly impatient.

"Yes, yes—he showed rather more courage than good sense. Lads of that age are often impetuous. And Julian, being younger than the others, no doubt feels a special need to keep his end up. I was of course appalled at the risk he ran. But a risk's not a bad thing now and then. There was an affair here last night. I don't know whether

149

you've heard of it—that represented a deliberate courting of risk. I was displeased about it, naturally. But I gather young Julian was all right on that, too."

Appleby nodded—and, as he did so, he dropped this elderly scholar into a certain pigeon-hole in his mind. "Do you know that fellow Farquharson?" he asked.

"No. He has no connection with my party whatever. A lonely man, I should imagine, retired from the Army rather early, with time on his hands and a nostalgic feeling for the charm of youth. A familiar type. Seldom any vice in it. But I don't think it can be said that he has a very well-stored mind."

Appleby had to take some care not to smile; it was once more a matter of characteristic academic attitudes. "The reading party," he asked, "consists simply of yourself and the undergraduates?"

"Dear me, yes. A Dr. Faircloth—whom I think you met on our extraordinary occasion this afternoon—has a little attached himself to us since he arrived the other day. My lads tell me he is a clergyman, but I find him to be a man of some learning. As a matter of fact, it was on his suggestion, and quite on the spur of the moment, that we decided on our late afternoon jaunt to Knack Tor. I had been working throughout the day—and have no doubt that most of the men believed themselves to have been doing that too—so the proposal was a pleasant one. Who could have believed how untoward the result would be! A deed of dreadful note. Or rather two of them."

"Three."

"Ah, yes." And Pettifor looked momentarily vague. "One really loses count. Things bad begun make strong themselves by ill. And may I ask, my dear Sir John, if you have any idea how these things came about?"

"Only a very general one. But perhaps it will serve for a

150

start. Henchman's body, you know—the one he came upon first—wasn't the same body that he and I found on the Tor later."

Pettifor got suddenly to his feet, crossed the room, and rang a bell. "I am forgetting the duties of hospitality," he said. "I hope I may offer you a drink. And this really sounds as if it requires one. I had no idea. But I now understand what you mean by three fatalities. Henchman has not been very explicit—but then he is, as I said, quite tired out. . . . But here is Lina." One of the George's engaging Italian maids had come into the room. "Brandy, perhaps, Appleby?"

Appleby accepted brandy. He also remarked this advance to a more familiar mode of address. "Henchman must have got to Knack Tor," he said, "round about noon. He appears to have been attracted to it by a column of smoke."

"Of smoke? How very unaccountable. It's not a time of year for heath fires."

"There's no heath up there, anyway. He formed a notion that what he saw might be a signal."

"A signal!" Pettifor was startled. "A kind of appeal for help?"

"Something of the sort. There can be little doubt that it was from a small fire kindled by a man who was presently shot dead. I have an idea myself that he may have been destroying papers."

"Here is the brandy. Armagnac—I hope that is all right? My friends maintain that it should always be taken in a warm cup from which one has just drunk the last of one's coffee. But I am perfectly content with a rummer myself. Ah, with the grape my fading life provide." And Pettifor took a first sniff at his brandy. "Now, what were you saying? Something about destroying papers."

151

"There is as yet no clue to the identity of the man whose body Henchman first found. But the body that he and I found later on I happened to have no difficulty in identifying. It was that of a man who had enjoyed a discreditable career in espionage—who worked, in fact, for two sides at once."

"I see." Pettifor took this not undramatic information coolly enough. "It scarcely sounds as if we need much mourn him. And do you suppose that the first man—the one who kindled the fire—was of the same kidney?"

"He may have been a victim rather than an associate. His death may have been the consequence of his resisting some demand or proposal." Appleby sipped his brandy. "That, of course, is a very tentative idea, but it's the direction in which my mind is moving."

"Most interesting. But I need hardly say that it takes me over ground entirely unfamiliar to me. Am I wrong in supposing that this conjecture of yours doesn't much assist to an understanding of why there was first one body and then another?"

Appleby nodded. "That's the core of the problem. And it certainly doesn't get me far with it."

Pettifor considered for a moment. "I said that David Henchman was a thoroughly reliable young man. And so he is. But could he, after all, have been perhaps mistaken? One body seems so much simpler than two."

"That's incontrovertible." Appleby spoke rather drily. "But I've never found I got far by ignoring awkward evidence. And this wasn't a matter of hurried glimpses. Henchman found a dead body, examined that dead body, and then, in the presence of that dead body, held quite a substantial conversation with another man. And the instant we returned to the Tor it was that other man's body that he declared to be lying there in front of us. We must accept it as gospel, I think, that the substitution of one body for another did, after some fashion, take place."

There was a short silence, and then Pettifor sighed rather helplessly. "You puzzle me sorely," he said.

At this moment the Italian maid returned to summon Pettifor to the telephone. He excused himself and went out, leaving Appleby with his nose buried thoughtfully in his rummer. David's tutor was certainly right in supposing that Appleby's conjectures weren't taking him very far. He could see no key to that enigmatical switching of the bodies. Hither hurried whence, and whither hurried hence? He frowned as this absurd jingle formed itself in his mind. He took a sip of the Armagnac.

> Another and another cup to drown
> The memory of this impertinence. . . .

Pettifor's habit of tags and snippets of verse was perhaps catching. Still, *whither* hurried hence? *Where* had that first body gone? And suddenly an extraordinary streak of light played upon the affair. He put down his rummer, and sat up with an exclamation. Then he rose and walked about the room, absorbed in thought. He hardly heard the door when it opened again, and it was a moment before he turned round, expecting to see Pettifor.

But it wasn't Pettifor who had come in. It was Dr. Faircloth—obscurely conjectured, he remembered, to be a clergyman.

"Good evening," Faircloth said. "Pettifor has asked me to make you his apologies. He has been called away—and, I fear, in considerable distress. There has been some sort of accident. His brother, I am sorry to say. . . . What a shocking day it has been with us! I am really rather relieved that my daughter hasn't been able to turn up."

153

2 "YOUR DAUGHTER WAS to have joined you?" Appleby thought it civil for a moment to continue this theme.

"Yes, my daughter Alice. She was to have motored from Hampshire, where she has been staying with friends. When she hadn't turned up by lunch-time, I was a little worried. However, there was a telegram later. I showed it to our friend David Henchman at dinner. I'm not supposed to know, but Pettifor's young men have been indulging in various conjectures about Alice. Many of them, I have no doubt, would be unsuitable for elderly ears." Faircloth, who was comfortably smoking a cigar, sat down opposite Appleby in an entirely companionable way. "Not that to-day's adventures haven't put Alice and everything else out of their delightful heads. These have been horrible events, my dear Sir John. They shock me profoundly. I am glad, as I say, that my child hasn't tumbled in upon them. But for the young men they represent a wonderful irruption of excitement and speculation. I am afraid that Plato and Kant and the rest of them will be very poor seconds for some days—and even if the mystery is cleared up at once. For I suppose it is a mystery? You would—expert in these matters as you are—accord it that status?"

Appleby could understand why Pettifor's youths had decided Faircloth was a clergyman. It wasn't just something vaguely suggestive in his name. He could find a good many words to cover no great quantity of matter. A few years ago, some of the young men had been surreptitiously timing such discourses in their school chapel, whether in the interest of winning wagers or merely compiling records. "A mystery?" he said. "I need make no bones about that. What happened on Knack Tor is at present completely inexplicable."

"Pettifor has no theory?"

"Well, he certainly hasn't advanced one." Appleby eyed Faircloth curiously. "Have you any theory yourself?"

"My dear sir, I'm not even in possession of the facts." And Faircloth suddenly raised a hand, as if anxious to forestall a flow of indiscreet communication. "Nor, I assure you, do I ask for them. I quite understand that matters of this sort, especially where national security is concerned, must be treated with the utmost circumspection. It is something I have been impressing—or endeavoring to impress—upon Colonel Farquharson. As a military man he ought, of course, already to be aware of it."

Appleby raised his eyes from his brandy—he had been letting it circle slowly round the glass—and regarded Faircloth more thoughtfully than he had yet done. "Farquharson?" he said presently. "Do you know much about him?"

"My dear sir, nothing at all. Remember that I have been in Nymph Monachorum only for a few days. And I don't think, indeed, that Farquharson is a man with whom I should readily become intimate."

"But you have nevertheless been discussing the affair with him this evening?" Appleby shook his head seriously. "May I be so impertinent, sir, as to offer you a word of

155

advice? Hold very little communication with him over this matter."

"Dear me!" Faircloth was impressed. "Would it be too venturesome to ask whether he is somebody already known to you?"

Appleby shook his head. "Not exactly that. And nobody concerned, I may say, was known to me before to-day, with the exception of Redwine, the man that Henchman and I found dead on Knack Tor. But I have been making what enquiries I could, both locally and by telephone to my own people in London."

"About the whole lot of us?" Faircloth appeared to find this idea amusing, for he took the cigar from his mouth in order to laugh the more unrestrainedly.

"I am afraid so. It is a very early piece of routine. Of course the connection between the events on the moor to-day and anybody in this hotel may be extremely tenuous. Henchman may be the only link—and a purely fortuitous one. Still, one does what one can. And one result has been the discovery that this Colonel Farquharson is not a person of estimable character."

"I am very sorry to hear it." Faircloth said this with a proper sobriety.

"Perhaps if you become conscious of anything out of the way in his conduct, you will be good enough to let me know."

"Certainly, certainly." Faircloth clearly regarded this proposed alliance with interest and satisfaction. "But is what you have heard about him—well, of likely relevance to our mystery? Does it in any way point a finger of suspicion at him?"

Appleby shook his head. "It isn't possible to go as far as that." He hesitated. "You understand, Dr. Faircloth, that all this is highly confidential?"

"By all means. And I may truly say that I support a very tolerable character for discretion."

For a moment Appleby was silent. He might have been admiring the oratundity of this last turn of phrase on Faircloth's part. Then he finished his brandy. "Not to put too fine a point on it," he said, "this man Farquharson is a professional blackmailer."

Faircloth received this confidence with notable *aplomb*. "My brief observation of Farquharson's bearing," he said, "would have inclined me rather to the supposition that he was a blackmailee. But perhaps I coin a word."

"If you do, it's a perfectly comprehensible one. And as blackmail is a crime, and a grave one, it is of course true that every blackmailer is potentially on every other blackmailer's list. Farquharson is, in fact, a convicted blackmailer; and they are commonly extremely cautious in their future operations. His presence down here may be entirely innocent."

Faircloth nodded. "And even if he is in Nymph Monachorum for what we may term professional purposes, are these at all likely to be related to our affair?"

"My guess is that they are. That secret meeting on Knack Tor, together with a sudden burning of what were in all probability some sort of papers, looks to me to belong within a context of blackmail." Appleby rose. "Anyway, I'm going to have a little conversation with Colonel Farquharson now."

"I believe you'll find him in his room. It's Number 10. He seems to work away at something there with a typewriter."

"Thank you. And I need hardly ask you to keep our discussion entirely between ourselves."

"My dear Sir John, you can rely on me. This is a most

157

distressing business, and I am only too anxious that it should be cleared up. And—do you know?—I am a little concerned about Pettifor. A delightful man, I judge. But sensitive, very sensitive. His young men's involvement in those terrible risks has upset him, I can see. And now some quite different trouble has come along. I shall be rather glad when we see him back."

If Appleby thought this solicitude for a very slight acquaintance remarkable, he didn't say so. "A brother?" he asked. "Living near here?"

"So I understand. And Pettifor has gone off in his car. I hope it doesn't let him down. He was having trouble with it this morning. I don't know why people run these elderly cars."

Appleby thought there was rather an obvious answer to this one, but that it didn't require embarking upon. "I think," he said, "that I'll try to persuade this Farquharson to take a little stroll. His kind are sometimes more communicative when they are sure there can be no eavesdroppers. And there's a moon. And the night's surprisingly mild."

Faircloth nodded. "I hope you will tell me what happens. I am most interested in what you have told me about Farquharson. He strikes me as promising. . . . Do you know, I believe I could become quite an amateur of crime?"

There was certainly a clatter of typewriting from Farquharson's room. Appleby knocked and walked in. The occupant was working at a small table piled with books and papers, and there were more of these on the bed. He turned and looked at Appleby sombrely but without any appearance of hostility. "Good evening," he said.

"Good evening, Colonel. You will remember me as a

little involved in the afternoon's operations. My name is Appleby."

"Yes, indeed. Sir John Appleby. Bad show, that. But might have been a damned sight worse."

"Decidedly. I hope I'm not interrupting you too inconveniently."

"No, no. I put in some time of an evening working at my regimental history. Not a regiment that ever did much in a spectacular way. But I was glad to take the job on. Whiles away the time of an evening."

"And by day you fish? Did you have good sport this morning?"

Farquharson took a moment to consider this. "I didn't take my rod out, as a matter of fact. Hung about, rather. Thought one of those lads might care for a tramp. But they were all hard at their books. Examinations ahead, it seems. I admire their application. Never much at it myself."

"I wonder whether you'd care for a short walk now?"

Farquharson didn't appear particularly surprised at this invitation—nor much gratified either. But he pushed his typewriter aside and stood up. "Very well," he said. "It's not a bad night. We might ask Pettifor, too. And any of his lads."

"Pettifor has gone off in his car. He's had bad news about a brother. And, as a matter of fact, Colonel, I thought you and I might have a confidential talk."

Farquharson gave what might have been a small sigh, and nodded. This proposal didn't seem to surprise him either. "Is it your idea," he asked, "that all this shooting is in some way connected with people in the hotel?"

"It's a possibility I have to consider." Appleby spoke cautiously. "You know how, for a start, Henchman walked straight into it."

"Straight would be the word, if you ask me. Nothing wrong with that boy."

"Probably not. But then there's another odd fact in the way the whole lot of you turned up later."

"At the kill, eh? Perfectly true." For a moment Farquharson appeared to give this careful consideration. "We might have been staging a sort of alibi—is that the word? Making it clear, I mean, that we weren't operating behind the scenes. It was that fellow Faircloth, I think, who suggested the jaunt. Not on your list of suspects, I'd suppose. They say he's a parson. Time on his hands, though. And that's not a blessing, believe me." And Farquharson took a restless turn about the room. "Overcoat? I think not."

They went downstairs and through the hall. Timothy Dumble and Arthur Drury were standing, tankards of cider in hand, before a map that hung on the wall. They appeared to be engaged, politely and obstinately, in some interminable topographical argument. Appleby nodded to them, and they looked at him curiously as he went past, but without addressing him. Outside, the moon was up in a clear sky, and the quiet village street appeared to be already asleep beneath it. Appleby walked a few paces with his companion, and then stopped. "Will you wait just a couple of minutes?" he asked. "I think I must have left my pipe in the smoking-room."

"Certainly. I'll just take a turn down to the bridge." Farquharson had produced a pipe of his own. "Surprisingly mild. Might be June."

Appleby hurried back to the George. The two young men were still standing before the map. "Come with me," he said briskly. "Both of you."

They followed him like a shot, and were half-way upstairs before Timothy Dumble ventured to ask a question. "Where to, sir?"

"Colonel Farquharson's room." Appleby had got out a pen-knife and was opening it. "As quick as we can."

"I say!" Timothy was delighted. "You want us as assistant burglars?"

"No. Only as witnesses—witnesses of quite a small job I have to do. A long shot, I'm afraid."

"Long shots are quite the go to-day, sir."

"Quite so. And this is another that mayn't come off. But it's worth trying, all the same. Mark what you see, gentlemen, but don't tell a soul."

Timothy nodded happily. "Mum's the word," he said. "And I'll see that Arthur here doesn't blab."

3 APPLEBY'S SHORT WALK, whether or not it was agreeable to Colonel Farquharson, didn't last long. The two men were back in the George within half an hour. And they parted at the foot of the staircase without a word.

Timothy Dumble was still in the hall. This time he was alone—sprawled across an armchair, and idly turning over the pages of a magazine. But as soon as Farquharson had vanished he spoke in a low voice. "I say, sir!"

Appleby strolled over to him and sat down. "Yes?"

"I don't know if I'm just making a fuss. The sort of alarms that have been happening to-day rather start one imagining things, I suppose. And when you, sir, set about playing odd tricks on retired military men—"

"Never mind about that." Appleby cut this apologetic rambling short. "Has something happened?"

"I don't know. But David isn't in his room. And he did go to bed. I know he did."

Appleby glanced quickly about him. "You've been to see?"

"Yes—just since you went out with that glum soldier. David's had the hell of a day, if you ask me, and it did just occur to me to stick my head in quietly and see that he was all tucked up and slumbering. He'd vanished."

Appleby frowned. "Lavatory—something like that?"

"I don't think so. I went back just five minutes ago, and there was still no sign of him."

"Clothes?"

"I didn't look." Timothy blushed, as if he felt that this was to have slipped up badly. "Or rather, I do remember that bluey was there."

Appleby was perplexed. "Bluey?"

"It's what he calls his old wind-cheater. And his shorts —I do remember now that they're on a chair. But, of course, he'd had a bath and changed before dinner."

"Come along." Appleby was on his feet, and he didn't look pleased. Timothy led him silently to David Henchman's room. The bed-clothes were thrown back. The wind-cheater and shorts were certainly on a chair. And David's pyjamas had been tossed on to a hook on the back of the door.

Timothy peered into a wardrobe. "Gent's pin-stripe still here," he said. "So he hasn't gone off in his glory. Cavalry twill bags and modest Old Boy's blazer vanished. That's it."

"How many of you are there?"

"Of Pettifor's lot? Five others. Ian, Tom, Arthur, Leon and the infant Ogg. I think they've all gone to bed now. Certainly Ian has. He's supposed to have done something silly to a shoulder."

"Go round the whole bunch—will you? But don't have them flocking round with cries. Bring any of them that knows anything along here. And tell the others to stay put."

"Aye, aye, sir." Timothy, who had been in the Navy, vanished at a soundless double. He was back within a few minutes. "None of them knows a thing. But Ian's vanished too."

"Dancer? Isn't he supposed to be laid up?"

"They've bandaged him or something. I suppose he can get about."

"And he's the one that David would—well, choose?"

"Him or me."

"What's the difference?"

Timothy considered this. "Ian would do madder things."

"I see." Appleby didn't look as if he thought this too good. "But you wouldn't say that David himself is harebrained?"

"Not a bit. But he can get it into his head that something's up to him. And then he's hopeless—absolutely pitiful." Timothy put a lot of commiseration into this. It was plain that he admired David Henchman. "Do you think his disappearance—and Ian's—is part of the mystery?"

"Well, not a mysterious part of it. I've a notion, that's to say, of what they're up to. But I don't know where they are—and, wherever it is, I don't know what pointer took them there. Has either of them got a car?"

Timothy shook his head. "No. But Ian has an arrangement with Leon Kryder—that's our quiet American—and can always borrow his motor-bike. Shall we go and look?"

They went downstairs and out into the inn yard. An old skittle-alley at the back had been converted into garage-space, but it was too narrow for the line of doors to close upon other than small cars. Timothy glanced into one empty space.

"Pettifor's not back yet. Somebody said something about an accident to his brother at Tremlett."

"Tremlett—what's that?"

"It's a manor house on the coast. Pettifor's elder brother's the squire there. Or he's that among other things. I've a notion he's eminent in some way. You can tell that

164

Pettifor's frightfully proud of him. I hope it isn't a bad accident. . . . By jove, that Faircloth type has taken his car out, too. And here's where Leon's bike's kept. Vanished, you see."

"Something of an exodus, in fact." Appleby glanced up at the windows of the George. They were now for the most part in darkness. "Surely Dancer couldn't drive a bike with a strapped-up shoulder?"

"Oh, David could make it go." Timothy paused for a moment, and then seemed to find something sinister in Appleby's silence. "I say! Is there anything we can do?"

"About these two young men? I'm afraid not. Or not directly and with any immediate effect. Which is bad."

"You think they'll get into danger or something?"

"I do." Appleby was unemotional. "And at the moment, it's just something they must take their chance of. I've no means whatever of running them speedily to earth. And I've got another job on hand."

Timothy Dumble was again silent. And when he did speak, it was in an anxiously casual way. "Can I help, by any chance?"

Appleby nodded. "Yes. You can."

There was little nocturnal traffic in these parts, and the moon-lit run to Tremlett took only half-an-hour. Appleby drove his car fast on the high road, but on leaving it for a narrow winding lane that dropped between high banks towards the sea his pace had been everything that safety required. So he certainly wasn't responsible, Timothy knew, for the accident that nearly overtook them. Up the hill and round a corner dead in front of them a car had come hurtling, without warning and without lights. They had scarcely realised its presence when the driver switched on a dazzling beam full in

their faces. Appleby swerved to the left so that the perpendicular earthen bank seemed to be grazing Timothy's
shoulder. There was a rush of air. The hurtling car was
behind them and had vanished round a bend.

"The unutterable ass!" Timothy appeared more indignant then alarmed. "Going along at that pace without
lights, and then losing his head and turning on that
bloody great beam."

"You didn't see the chap?"

"Good lord, no."

"Nor even what make of car it was? No more did I."
And Appleby laughed. "We can't get him for dangerous
driving, I'm afraid. Just take the torch and have another
look at the map. Could he have been coming from anywhere except Tremlett?"

"The road goes a little farther along the coast, with
tracks going down to two or three coves before it peters
out. He may have been having quiet fun—or just inter-
course with nature—down one of them."

"Very possibly." Appleby sounded sceptical. "Do you
know the house?"

"Absolutely not. I've never been near the place. Pettifor
doesn't make it one of the sights. Rather shy, I think,
about his brother the squire."

"Why should he be that?"

"I haven't a clue. Over-compensating for inwardly feeling grand about him, perhaps." Timothy produced this
fragment of modern psychology with some pride. "If these
contours aren't just filled in according to fancy, the house
must be quite a bit above the shore. There ought to be a
short drive about five hundred yards ahead. I can smell
the sea."

"I expect you could hear it, too, if we stopped. It seems
never really still on this coast. Rocks and coves and cur-

rents and general restlessness. The unslumbering sea. Tricky." Appleby slowed down. "That must be the drive. And I think I can just see the house against the sky. Only the upper storeys, probably. No lights."

The car turned in between stone pillars and past what seemed to be an untenanted lodge. A short run brought it to the house, and Appleby drew up. Except for a single light under a porch, the whole place was in darkness. And now they could certainly hear the sea.

"Not very cheerful, is it?" Timothy asked as he climbed out. "Hullo, there's Pettifor's car—our Pettifor, I mean. So he's still here, all right."

The Land Rover was a little farther along the sweep. They walked to the porch together, and found that it sheltered what must be the front door. Appleby rang a bell. It was an old-fashioned affair, and they could hear it clang in some distant place. They waited.

Nothing happened. There was no light and no sound. Appleby rang again, and again they waited with no result. "I think we'll take a walk round," Appleby said.

They walked down the sweep and round a corner. The moonlight showed up the house in substantial detail. It seemed large and venerable and architecturally undistinguished. The sound of the sea was louder and had taken on specific character. They could tell that down below small insistent waves were breaking over rock.

Appleby stopped. "Voices."

There were certainly voices, but they seemed very far away. They were distinguishable and then faded out again as if carried by a veering wind.

"A light," Timothy said, and pointed along the pale shimmer of the façade by which they stood. The light seemed to be streaming from an uncurtained window. They walked on. They were on a bare terrace with a low

167

balustrade. Beyond it there was a small garden sloping steeply away, and traversed by paths which eventually dipped and disappeared as if in some steeper drop towards the sea. The tang of the sea was in the air. "A french window," Timothy said. "And it's open."

Appleby stepped forward and without diffidence studied the lighted room. It was large and furnished as a library. Not—one could tell at once—the sort of library that moulders undisturbed from generation to generation in many large houses, but a library that was fully functional. There wasn't much furniture. A handsome desk stood uncompromisingly in the centre of the room. The only ornament was a life-sized bronze figure of a youth, stripped and in the attitude of a diver, that stood in one corner.

"Our Pettifor's hat." Timothy pointed to a chair. "But the whole place seems deserted."

"Listen." Appleby had turned away from the room and towards the sea. "Those voices again. They must be down by the shore. The whole household, servants and all. That's the explanation."

"And our Pettifor's joined them?"

"Precisely. I think we'd better join them too."

4 THEY MOVED ACROSS the terrace and descended a flight of steps to the garden. Somewhere there was already lilac in flower; its scent mingled with that of rock pools and sea wrack. "There's the sea," Timothy said. "It's quite calm and still."

The water lay like an empty mirror. There was a single line of lights very far away, like a faint gilding on an invisible frame. "It's calm out there," Appleby said. "But listen to it nosing round down below. Here's the path to the cove."

They dropped down by a tumble of rock; the voices had faded again and there was only the plash of small waves and the patter of falling spray. In an inlet straight beneath them the sea was rising and falling like a breathing thing. Timothy scanned the rocks. "Nobody. Nobody at all."

"There must be a series of these coves. We'll go on." Appleby pointed. "The path runs that way."

The next cove was empty, too. The path dropped down to it and a thin drift of spray blew over them. "A boat," Timothy said. "There—beyond the point." There was a rowing-boat, with a figure resting on the oars. A man stood in the stern. He seemed to be gesturing to the empty night.

Appleby watched him. "It's the next. We'll have to climb up again. And there are the voices."

As they scrambled upwards they could hear men calling to each other—sparely and with a strange effect of solemnity—across the water. The next cove was larger, and larger waves seemed to be rolling into it. There was a sliver of sand. A small group of people, men and women, stood on it, gazing out to sea. A hundred yards out were two more boats, rowing slowly side by side. And even as they watched a figure detached itself from the group and moved towards them—slowly, unsteadily, and stumbling on the rock.

"It's Pettifor. Had we better go back?" Timothy spoke awkwardly, as if he were only just realising what it was all about.

Appleby shook his head, and a moment later Pettifor was on the path before them. He halted. It was impossible to tell whether he was startled, or almost unaware of their presence. When he spoke, it might have been to himself. "They never will," he said. "They have to try. But they never will. Never, never, never, never, never."

They followed him silently back to the house. On the terrace Appleby dropped back for a moment and murmured to Timothy Dumble. "Could you drive my car?"

"Yes. I'm sure I could."

"Then get back to the George in it. There's just a possibility for some message from your precious couple on the motor-bike. If there is, use your judgment."

Timothy made off with alacrity; he clearly didn't know how to behave to a man who could quote *King Lear* like that. It was as indecent as would have been a command

170

to howl, howl, howl, howl. He was fond of Pettifor. But that made it only the more embarrassing.

The two men went into the lighted library. Pettifor picked up his hat and stared at it absently. "My brother's drowned," he said.

Appleby walked across the room and looked at the figure of the diving youth. "He was fond of the sea?"

"Passionately. And a strong swimmer. But that sometimes makes a man foolhardy. Poor Arthur! He'll never take a book from these shelves again. And no children—any more than I have. It's the end of us"—he made a small resigned gesture—"and that's a thing hard to realise. For there have been Pettifors at Tremlett for quite a long time."

"They know it was down there? And they're trying to recover the body now?"

"Yes. Arthur's clothes were there. They've been at it since the late afternoon. But they'll never recover the body —never. Not with the currents as they are hereabouts. It makes all bathing dangerous."

Appleby was silent for a moment. Not even long professional experience made him easy in questioning a man who was overcome with grief. And Pettifor was certainly that. He had the dazed air of one who is beginning to emerge from the first anaesthetic effect of a major shock. When Appleby did speak it was mildly. Nevertheless his words produced a startling effect. "Isn't it very early in the year for anything of the sort?"

"For God's sake don't let your mind start running that way!" Pettifor made another gesture, as if he were repelling some physical menace. "I know it's your element; I know you've come straight from that strange, violent business of this afternoon. And I know, too, that men sometimes contrive the appearance of this sort of thing.

But I am quite—"

"Of this sort of thing?" Appleby seemed puzzled. "I don't follow you."

"If a man—a man of our sort—feels he must take his own life, he will at least try to contrive something to relieve his end of the certainty of disgrace. He'll go out and have an accident with his gun while getting over a stile. Or he'll do what you may be thinking Arthur has done. But it just isn't so. Arthur would never commit suicide. I can tell you that on my honour as a gentleman."

Appleby received these strange words with a bow. It didn't seem possible to find an articulate reply that would be much to the point. "Your brother," he asked, "was accustomed to go swimming at any time?"

"Arthur was pretty well an all-the-year-round man. The estate takes in a long stretch of the coast, you know, and it's entirely secluded. From boyhood he's had the habit of a quick dip in the course of a ramble. But his favourite cove is that one, quite near the house. "Was that one, I ought to say." Abruptly, Pettifor sank down on a chair. "I wish they'd give over," he said. "It's nothing but a mockery."

Appleby had turned away from the statue and was making a casual survey of the shelves that ran all round the library. "Did your brother," he asked, "live here all the time?"

"No, not all the time." Pettifor spoke dully. "Didn't you bring one of my lads—Dumble?" He got to his feet again. "Drinks," he said vaguely. "It falls on me now, I suppose—all that sort of thing. And, anyway, Arthur would have wished—"

He had opened a cupboard, and there was a glimpse of bottles and glasses. Appleby shook his head. "Thank you, no. And I've sent the young man back to Nymph Monachorum in my car. I thought it was the best place for him . . . while we had some conversation."

"Conversation?" Pettifor still seemed bewildered, but he managed to say this a little stiffly. "Is it exactly the time for that?"

"I'm rather afraid it precisely is."

Pettifor took a turn about the room. "Unbidden guests," he murmured, "are often welcomest when they are gone." Then he flushed. "I beg your pardon. What an extraordinary thing to say!"

Appleby smiled. "The poets have a word for every occasion, haven't they? And, of course, you are absolutely right, sir. There must be an inquest, and so on, on your brother's death; and no doubt the county police will have to come and make inquiries. But I have no business here at all. If you want me to go, I'll go."

Pettifor passed a hand through his sparse hair. He had the appearance of ageing with the tick of the clock. "Stay—stay, for heaven's sake. There's deep water in this." He stopped again, as if this image were an awkwardly poignant one. "Look here, Appleby—have you anything in your mind?"

Appleby considered this; he found it impossible to decide whether its tone constituted an appeal or a challenge. "I think," he said presently, "it would be fair to say this: I've got in my mind already what will shortly be in the minds of other people who come along." He paused. "And perhaps one or two other things as well. I suppose you are your brother's heir?"

"His heir?" Pettifor took the abrupt question merely stupidly.

"You inherit Tremlett—your family home?"

"Yes, yes." Pettifor relapsed into vagueness again. "But

what's the use of it to me? My life has shaped itself in other places. Very good places, if it comes to that. What should I do here—talk to farmers, and see to barns and gates and fences? I could bring my young men here, I suppose, instead of to Nymph Monachorum." He gave a bleak smile. "And they could play chicken on the cliffs. . . . But I never shall." Pettifor paused, as if suddenly struck by something wholly puzzling. "Why do you ask this—about who inherits, and so forth?"

"Call it routine. Certainly it's a sort of question that does get asked . . . when the owner of substantial property disappears."

"Disappears?" Pettifor's perplexity grew. "But Arthur hasn't disappeared! You speak as if there were something sinister about his death—which is absurd."

"It has at least followed hard upon indubitably sinister events, not far away. And remember, please, I'm only thinking the thoughts of your local police, as these will be made quite clear to you when they arrive. I assure you that they won't, for one thing, ignore the possibility of suicide. On the contrary, they'll take up the several causes that commonly drive a man that way, and they'll conduct a thorough investigation to discover whether any of them applies. You can guess what they are: incurable disease, great pain, marital difficulties, financial difficulties, threat of some exposure or disgrace, blackmail, severe depression or other nervous disturbance, unbearable bereavement, the consciousness or persuasion of failing intellectual powers—"

"For heaven's sake, stop!" Pettifor again contrived his bleak smile. "Leave something to the imagination, man."

"Of course there's a great difference between suspecting all sorts of things, and proving a single one of them. You've no doubt been struck by that."

"I haven't been struck by that, or anything else. You speak as if I'd had leisure to sit down and think about my brother's death in all its most unlikely aspects. When I do have time for reflection, it will be along less fantastic lines, I should suppose. Tremlett, for instance. I'm deeply attached to the place, as you can guess. But it's going to be a mere headache, as the young men say, to a person of my habits and temperament. I don't delude myself about that."

"May I ask what will happen to the property after your own death?"

Pettifor stared. "It will go to my sister's son, I suppose."

"The boy I've met—Julian Ogg?"

"Yes, to Julian. He'll be all right."

"I'm sure he will. And perhaps he'll take the name of Pettifor? It's a distinguished name."

Pettifor seemed not very much gratified by this. "There's nothing wrong with the name—and it's of some antiquity, if that's of any significance. But I don't know that it's made much noise in the world."

Appleby shook his head. "The name of Arthur Pettifor means something to me," he said.

5 "YOU SURPRISE ME. Arthur lived a quiet sort of life." Pettifor had fallen to pacing up and down the dead man's library. "A civil servant, you know."

"Always?"

"Well, he was what might be called a week-end squire down here. He couldn't manage much more than that."

Appleby shook his head. "That's not what I meant. He went into the civil service late?"

"Oh, certainly. Arthur had a scientific training. Like so many fellows, he went into the civil service in a temporary way during the war. But he decided to stay. It surprises me that you should know about him."

"Well, I do—a little. And I found out rather more, when I was making a number of enquiries on the telephone before dinner."

Pettifor frowned. "You don't waste time. Arthur hadn't entered the picture then."

"Ah—so you do now feel he's in it?" Appleby asked this mildly. "In any case, you were, you know. So I thought I'd just freshen up on your brother."

"Freshen up on him?" Pettifor flushed. "Are you suggesting that you ever had any professional concern with him before?"

Appleby shook his head. "Please be patient. And let your patience extend to going back to the idea of suicide."

"I tell you, sir—"

Appleby held up his hand. "I know you feel very strongly about its blank impossibility. But suppose it not impossible. Set aside your conviction, and grant me that. It is necessary to admit that one of those promptings to suicide that I was detailing to you might apply in your brother's case?"

For a moment Appleby thought that he was going to be turned out of Tremlett there and then. But Pettifor, although this time he flushed more darkly, answered quietly enough. "You mentioned marital difficulties. Well, my brother's marriage was dissolved. But that was many years ago now."

"His emotional constitution was not altogether normal?"

"Arthur was a man of the strictest and highest moral principles." Pettifor now spoke hotly. "Nobody has ever questioned it."

"Nevertheless the dissolution of his marriage had perhaps some painful background which has never been fully revealed?"

"That is so. His bride left him—she was not a woman who would have made a man a satisfactory wife in any circumstances—and later suffered a breakdown during which she embarked upon a course of deeply culpable conduct which I need not particularise. And her end was a most unhappy one. Unfortunately the tragedy never healed itself in my brother's mind. He became with the years only the more morbidly sensitive about it. It was the occasion of his going very little into society, and seldom receiving guests here at Tremlett. He felt himself—although utterly without justification—to be deeply responsible and disgraced."

177

"And all this, you say, about circumstances which never became fully public?"

"That is so."

"Surely, Mr. Pettifor, you realise that you are describing to me what is virtually the classical background to blackmail?"

"Perhaps so. But you are talking nonsense, nevertheless. If my brother had been twenty times blackmailed, Sir John, he would not have taken his own life. He might have come to the brink of it. But he would not have done it."

"I see." It was Appleby's turn to pace the length of the library. "Would it surprise you to learn that there is a known blackmailer staying in your hotel now?"

"Holding the opinion I do, I cannot be interested in whether there is or not."

"Well, there is." Appleby was now gazing into an empty fireplace, and he spoke without turning round. "A little time ago, you gave me your word of honour—on a matter of faith or conviction. Well, I give you my word of honour on a matter of sober fact. You have been in conversation with an extremely ruthless blackmailer this afternoon."

Pettifor made a restless movement. "Must this go on? The deep of night is crept upon our talk."

Appleby turned round. "Do you know, it's sometimes very dangerous to quote the poets? But I agree we've talked enough. Action may get us further. Will you allow me to search this room?"

"To search this room?" Pettifor was astounded.

"Certainly. And I'd propose to begin with your brother's desk, if I hadn't suddenly become rather more interested in this fireplace. Will you come over here?"

Pettifor strode across the room. "I've no idea what you're talking about," he said.

"No fire—just those two big logs. I suppose the place is centrally heated, and that there's a fire only in winter? Your brother seems to have had excellent servants." And Appleby glanced around the room. "Everything in order, and not a speck of dust. So they wouldn't, I think, have left that very long." And Appleby pointed into the hearth. "Would you agree, by the way, that I couldn't have contrived that effect myself?"

Pettifor followed the direction of Appleby's finger. "Not unless you came in here earlier."

"Ah—I was with young Timothy Dumble when I peered in here before meeting you. So this isn't a matter of a wicked policeman planting clues. If this is a clue, that is to say. We may be looking at a mare's nest. But it's worth investigating. Don't you agree?"

"That little heap of ashes and charred paper?" Pettifor's voice was now perplexed and uneasy. "I don't know what you mean."

"Can you honestly say that?" Appleby spoke drily. "Here we are, sir, talking about blackmail and suicide. And there, behind those logs in the grate, are some hastily destroyed papers. These are elements that compose together very readily, you know. I'm not sure I haven't met them to-day already."

"You talk in riddles. If there's anything that can be fished out of the hearth, fish it out. And then search the room if it pleases you."

Without a word Appleby stepped forward and fished in the fireplace. Pettifor watched him gloomily. What had been burnt appeared to be a few crumpled papers. One of these was imperfectly consumed; Appleby picked up the unburnt part carefully, carried it to the desk, and smoothed it out. The two men looked at it in silence. It was a triangular fragment, bearing a few lines of typescript, thus:

179

> *will*
> *you £2000 in*
> *this to the summit*
> *Tor punctually at noon*
> *and see that you come alone.*

The silence continued. Pettifor seemed stupefied; he walked away and stared through the French window into the night. Very faintly, the sound of the sea washed into the room. "I don't believe it," he said presently. "Two thousand pounds! There's no sense in it."

"There's a great deal of sense in it." Appleby had produced a pocket magnifying-glass and was examining the scrap of typescript carefully. "There's a great deal of enlightenment. It takes us right out of the dark."

Pettifor turned round. "I think it takes us straight into it. Darkness and disgrace. Oh, my God!"

"However that may be, we can now start getting one or two things clear. You will admit, Mr. Pettifor, that your brother met his death this morning on Knack Tor?"

"I will admit nothing, sir. Nor be questioned further. This interview must now end."

Appleby said nothing. He reached across the desk for a clean envelope, and carefully inserted into it the fragment of typescript. "The moving finger writes," he murmured.

"I beg your pardon?"

"Nor all thy piety nor wit shall lure it back to cancel half a line."

Pettifor frowned. "I'd expect my pupils," he said, "to amuse themselves from time to time by imitating my mannerisms—although scarcely in my presence. But that you, sir—"

"I'm sorry. But there's always, you know, some sort of associative process at work, is there not, when one seems to indulge in random quotation?" Appleby tapped the envelope. "It's certainly true that nothing will cancel what's written here. Do you remember, by any chance, the first occasion during our acquaintance upon which you quoted a scrap of the *Rubáiyát?*"

"I do not. And I can't think what this idle talk is leading to."

"It was very much a scrap. I didn't, indeed, catch on to it. It was only later, when I found the poem running in my own head, that it came to me, and that I realised I had caught something odd in your words. The occasion was this. You were remarking on your impression that David Henchman in fact knew the identity of the man whose body he and I found this afternoon on Knack Tor, but that he would not discuss the matter, so that you were still ignorant of the man's identity yourself. And what you said to me was: 'David's lips are locked.' It was pretty clearly a tag from something—but I didn't, as I say, catch on to it. However, I can quote the stanza now. Shall I do so?"

Pettifor had turned pale. "You can do as you please," he said shortly.

"Very well:

'And David's lips are locked; but in divine
High piping Pehlevi, with "Wine! Wine! Wine!
Red Wine!"—the nightingale cries to the rose
That yellow cheek of hers to incarnadine.'

You knew the man's name as well as I did. And by a trick of association you betrayed yourself."

There was a long silence before Pettifor spoke. "This is quite fantastic," he said.

"On the contrary, Mr. Pettifor, it is quite conclusive.

You had—and have—information which you were deter-mined to conceal. This man Redwine was found shot dead in circumstances which led directly to an affray in which the lives of your pupils—and particularly the life of your own nephew, Julian Ogg—were put at imminent hazard. And yet you remained silent on something which you knew about him: his name. That is an act of extraordinary ir-responsibility. You must have had some very grave motive for it."

"It is perfectly true." Pettifor sank down on a chair.

"And I think you have realised for some time that the whole obscure situation has developed in a way that you have no hope of controlling. The death of Redwine, the death of the man who was killed in Timothy Dumble's car this afternoon, the inescapable fact that some sort of ruth-less blackmail has been going on, information which I have myself acquired about your brother: these all represent, in your own words, deep water which you have no chance of keeping afloat in. The time has come for a show-down, has it not?"

Pettifor had buried his head in his hands. Now he raised it again. "Yes," he said. "I believe it has." Slowly he put a hand in a pocket and brought out a wallet. "And for the production of another document." He broke off suddenly. "What's that?"

There was a sound of running footsteps on the terrace, and a moment later Timothy burst into the room. "Ian," he panted. "I've found him."

Appleby swung round. "He's here?"

"Yes—I've got him in your car. He's done up."

"And David?"

"He went on. He went on when Ian had to drop out. On the motor-bike, I mean. But he knows where David's mak-ing for, so I thought I'd better bring him back here and collect you, sir."

"Quite right." Appleby turned to Pettifor and pointed to the wallet. "What you have there may be vital," he said. "But it will keep. So put it away, please, and come along."

"Come along?"

"Certainly. This is the crisis. Particularly for David Henchman. He's in danger—deadly danger."

"Good God!" Pettifor sprang to his feet. "I shall never forgive myself if—"

"Probably not. But you have a pat phrase for it, have you not? Things bad begun make strong themselves by ill." And Appleby glanced at Timothy as he hurried across the room. "You have the hang of this?"

Timothy, who was still panting, seemed bewildered. "Ian's nattering about a girl."

"Exactly. And we've got to find her."

6 Once more Appleby's car was rushing through the night. And once more Timothy Dumble was studying the map. "Yes," he said, "here it is. Farthing Bishop. About eight miles. It seems a tiny place."

"It must have a post office, anyway." From the back of the car, Ian Dancer spoke in the carefully controlled voice of somebody in pain.

"So it must—if your whole story's not crackers." Timothy paused. "You just had to get off?" he asked cautiously.

"No help for it. I was rocking about on the back of the bike, and wrecking the whole show. The beastly doctors were right. I thought they were talking rot."

"It was madness, Ian." Pettifor, also at the back, steadied the injured youth as the car swung round a corner.

"I thought I'd be all right, just hanging on behind. But the bloody thing made me howl whenever we bumped. David had to stop. And then we decided he must go on to this Farthing Bishop place by himself. I sat by the roadside for a bit, and managed to get a cigarette going. That made me feel a lot better. I began to think I'd been damned soft not to hold on. Then I saw I must get somewhere where I could get hold of the police and tell them about David."

"Did you, indeed?" Appleby, intent over the wheel,

184

spoke grimly. "It was a somewhat belated thought, if I may say so."

"I'm sorry. Well, I managed to get on my feet again and reach the high road. I thought I'd thumb something. And what I was lucky enough to thumb was Timothy here in your car, making back to Nymph Monachorum. We decided the best thing was to turn round and contact you at Tremlett."

"You were quite right. But what about the start of the business? Just what put it into your thick heads—yours and David Henchman's—to go off into the blue without a word?"

"Hear, hear!" Timothy didn't seem to feel that his friend's agony deserved much consideration. "Why didn't you tell me, you low hound?"

"You?" Ian was scornful. "That would have meant the whole gaggle in an instant. I expect we'd have told Sir John, if we'd known he was at the George."

"And just what would you have told me? What put his notion about the girl in David's mind? Was it something Faircloth said?"

"It was a little more than that, sir. You see, the old boy had been expecting his daughter all day, and she just hadn't turned up."

"But didn't he have a telegram?"

"That was later. Actually, it was the telegram that gave David his suspicion of the truth. Or rather, it was the telegram that strengthened it. He had a first glimpse of the thing when he was having a bath before dinner."

"I see." Appleby's voice was patient. "Of course there's nothing more reliable than the sort of sudden notion that comes to one in a hot bath after an utterly exhausting day. Go on."

"He suddenly had this awful idea that it might have

185

been poor old Faircloth's precious Alice that he had encountered in that car this morning. You see, she was supposed to be motoring over from friends in Hampshire. She might quite easily have taken the road over the moor, and have stopped to picnic near Knack Tor. And so it would have been her car that David's pursuers stole. And that would account for her not turning up in Nymph Monachorum."

Pettifor interrupted. "It would only account, surely, for her not turning up in the car."

"But you see, sir, David realised that there might be an even more sinister side to it. These chaps were pursuing him simply to prevent their ever being identified by him and connected with what had happened up on the Tor. Well the girl must have had a perfectly clear sight of them when they bagged her car. So anything might happen."

"It might, indeed," Appleby said. "And that was as far as David's thoughts got in his bath?"

"Yes. And then at dinner there was old Faircloth, quite relieved in his mind. As far as Alice was concerned, I mean. Of course he was upset about all the horrors of the day. But he'd had this telegram from the girl, saying she was stopping in Hampshire a bit longer. So that seemed all right. And then David went to bed."

"It's a pity he didn't stay there. What got him out again?"

"He'd happened to notice the name of the post office where the telegram had been handed in. It was Farthing Bishop. And suddenly, just as he was dropping off to sleep, he remembered seeing Farthing Bishop on the map—the local map—and being told something about it. It's not in Hampshire; it's quite close by. No doubt Faircloth hadn't noticed. It's not a thing one always does notice on a telegram. But it meant the message must be false. Alice had been kidnapped or something by the enemy gang. David

186

came and explained it all to me."

"Explained is precisely the word. And then?"

"Well, we boggled over it rather. It seemed possible and not possible. We wondered whether we should search out old Faircloth and reveal our suspicions. I was rather for doing that. But David seemed to feel it was up to him personally to go right in and find the girl. He had a notion he'd rather let her down. So we decided to borrow Leon's bike and go and reconnoitre Farthing Bishop."

"And David is presumably there now. Do you know anything about it?"

"Nothing at all. But Colonel Farquharson was saying something about it yesterday—I think that the manor house is untenanted."

"Quite right." Pettifor, who had remained for the most part sunk in sombre silence, contributed this. "People called Hotchkiss. They departed some years ago, being too hard up for the place, and have never been able to find a tenant. Indeed, it's partly ruined, and there's a tower of great antiquity."

"It sounds," Appleby said, "a striking object in the landscape, even by moonlight. Owls and ivy, I suppose, and everything thoroughly romantic."

"No doubt. But I never heard there was anything romantic about the Hotchkisses. They were city people. I never knew them, and I don't think I know anybody in the neighbourhood either."

"David and I," Ian said, "wondered whether Colonel Farquharson did. I mean, whether he knows people near there. Because he shot past us."

"What's that?" Appleby's question came sharply.

"On this road, and just before I had to give up because of my shoulder. He overtook us in his car, going at a good lick. We'd drawn into the side, so he didn't see us."

"I say! Do you think it was just coincidence?" Timothy put this question with lively interest. "It seems to me there's a general convergence on this Farthing Bishop." He appealed to Appleby. "Don't you think so, sir?"

"I certainly do." Appleby's tone was grim. It was clear he hadn't greatly liked the news about Farquharson.

"Nobody missing except old Faircloth."

"Faircloth? You needn't worry. He certainly got there some time ago. He was making for the place when he passed us."

"Passed us?" Timothy was bewildered.

"My dear lad, the car that nearly ran into us as we were approaching Tremlett was certainly Faircloth's."

At this Pettifor sat forward. "Appleby, what was that? Faircloth at Tremlett! Whatever should he be doing there?"

"He had some quiet business to transact."

"Business!"

"Yes. But, oddly enough, its true nature wasn't clear to him."

"Indeed." Pettifor didn't receive this enigmatic statement very patiently. "But no doubt it is perfectly clear to yourself?"

"Well, yes—as a matter of fact it is. And I hope to explain it to Faircloth quite soon. There isn't, you see, much mystery left in this affair. Only danger. And I was saying to David Henchman this morning that danger's not really so interesting. However, we must try to cope with it when it turns up."

There was danger, Timothy thought, simply in the pace they were travelling. And it was almost possible to believe that Appleby was relieving some state of nervous tension by talking at random. Timothy took a sidelong glance at him in the dim light. His face was set and stern.

188

Suddenly Timothy found himself lurching forwards. Appleby had braked powerfully, and now he brought the car to a halt. Timothy looked at him in surprise—and was yet more surprised to see that he was smiling broadly. "Well," Appleby said, "that's that. Didn't you see?"

"See, sir?"

Without answering, Appleby switched on a spot-light at the tail of the car and reversed. They ran back for about thirty yards, with Timothy staring out into the moonlight. By the side of the road a wheel came into view. And then a motor-bike. And then, standing by the machine and scowling furiously, David Henchman.

Timothy had lowered a window. Appleby leant across him. "Can we give you any help?" he called out cheerfully.

David stared at them. It was a second before he made them out. "It's stopped," he said. "It won't go. I've been here for ages."

"Perhaps we might take you on tow?" Appleby's voice held something that puzzled Timothy for a moment. And then he realised that it was simple joy. It was almost as if he hadn't expected to see David again.

"A tow? Don't be stupid." David was obviously dead tired as well as feeling a fool. "It's the beastly ignition. The thing won't fire." There was a moment's silence as David fiddled again with the machine. "Oh, good lord!" he said.

Appleby laughed aloud. "Petrol?"

"Yes. The tank's bone dry." David turned to him. One could see in the moonlight that he was flushed and furious. "Can you let me have some?"

"I could—certainly." Appleby was now quite grave again. "And then you could proceed on your own. And to the moated grange, I suppose."

"What do you mean—the moated grange?" David peered into the car, and spotted Ian as well as Timothy. "What have these great idiots been saying?"

"They've been helping me to piece things together, I admit. And now you turn up like a bad penny. It's most satisfactory. Quite suddenly, this whole messy business comes under control. I think you'd better leave your friend's motor-bike—it will be safe enough where it is for an hour—and get in here. It would be a shame if you never saw that grange at all."

"I don't know what you're talking about." David still sounded sulky. But he was opening the door of the car and getting in beside Timothy.

"Haven't you been told that Farthing Bishop boasts a highly romantic deserted manor house, which even incorporates a lofty and ancient ivy-clad tower?"

"Yes, I did remember something of the sort, when I started thinking about the place. I must have heard it talked about lately. But I don't see—"

But Appleby had let in the clutch. "We must be getting on," he said. "My own curiosity about Farthing Bishop grows. You know, there's been a lot of artistry in this affair."

Pettifor leant forward sharply from the back. "Artistry? Just what do you mean?"

"Perhaps I ought to say a great deal of inspired improvisation. David jumping on Ian's horse, for instance, and then thinking to get himself smuggled away in an ambulance."

David laughed. His sulking fit wasn't proof against this memory. "It didn't work," he said.

"Quite so. And there's a lot more that isn't going to work, either."

7

THEY DROVE ON for some miles. "The house is on this side of the village," Timothy said, looking up from the map. "And it's marked in Gothic lettering. So it must be an antiquity." He turned round to Pettifor with a cheerful grin. "We ought to have brought the whole lot, sir. You could have expounded it to us."

Pettifor didn't seem to think much of this as a sally. And Timothy, suddenly remembering about Arthur Pettifor, was much abashed.

"I should imagine it's just the tower that's the antiquity," Appleby said. Suddenly he took a hand from the wheel and pointed. "And there it is."

There, certainly, was the tower. A turn of the road had revealed it set boldly against the sky-line, with the moon almost directly above it. And a moment later they could see the bulk of the house. Pettifor leant forward curiously. "I believe the tower is all that remains of a small mediaeval stronghold, and that it is in some reasonable state of preservation. Everything else is gone. No doubt the present mansion was quarried out of the ruins."

Appleby was slowing down. "An arresting sight," he murmured. "Calculated to strike the imagination at once. David—don't you agree?"

"I suppose so."

"And isn't that a light—a very faint light, high up? I think it is. Even if there's glass up there, I don't think a trick of moonlight would give that effect. Exciting, David— wouldn't you say?"

"Oh, shut up!" David appeared to feel that his day's adventures with Appleby entitled him to this amount of free expression. But then he continued, politely but urgently. "I don't believe you understand, sir. It may be most frightfully critical. You see—"

"I understand, all right." Appleby had brought his car to a stop. "And there's still a job for you to do." He paused, as if this utterance had brought up a fresh consideration. "Listen," he said. "There's something I want to say to you all." He had switched off the engine and there was suddenly complete silence all around them. It was preserved until Appleby spoke again. "This has been a perplexed business. I think I've seen my way through it. But one man's notion isn't much to take into court. Certain action, therefore, is necessary, if we are to be sure of seeing it satisfactorily cleared up. . . . Mr. Pettifor, the centre of all this is, of course, your brother's death. Will you give me your assurance that you want the circumstances of that death fully elucidated?"

There was a long silence, in which Pettifor's pupils might have been felt as going stiff with astonishment at this strange question and the blankness which succeeded upon it. But at length Pettifor spoke. "Yes," he said. "I give you that assurance."

"Thank you. And now we all get out." Appleby spoke briskly. "Except Dancer. He'd better stay put."

"What utter rot!" Ian was indignant. "I can get along as well as anybody. It was only that bloody bone-shaking bike."

192

"Very well. It's your own affair." Appleby gave the young man an appraising glance. "Only understand this: we are walking into a situation in which it may be desirable to be tolerably able-bodied. Got that?"

"I've got it." And Ian climbed from the car with elaborate ease.

Timothy jumped out too. "Sir," he said challengingly, "just what is the situation?"

Appleby smiled. "I'm not able to be too precise. Some friends of ours are here, I don't doubt. There's the retired clergyman of ample means, and there's the admirer of England's young manhood. There may be others as well. But their relative situations at the moment I'm afraid I can't describe. We now advance on foot."

Ian took a few experimental steps. "Nothing in it," he said. "I could do a mile." His dark eyes flashed in a face drained of colour by the moonlight. "Is this an attack?"

"It's a surprise attack, if that can be managed." Appleby pointed to the side of the road. "Single file, and as much in shadow as possible. No talking. There'll be a drive. We'll stop there to reconnoitre."

"Do you mean," David asked, "that we're all going together? You said there was a job for me. Do you mean just in the crowd?"

"No, I don't. I mean something rather risky. You might call it One Man Chicken."

"I see." David was now too seasoned a campaigner to greet this with pleased excitement. "An infant Ogg turn? Valley of death stuff?"

"Certainly not as bad as that. Remember their prize marksman's dead. And now—straight ahead."

They walked silently down the road, with Appleby leading. Both house and tower had disappeared behind a line of trees on their left, and presently they passed a lane running off to their right, with a signpost announcing that the village of Farthing Bishop lay half-a-mile in front of them. The trees grew thicker and seemed to stretch interminably ahead. And then suddenly there was a gap, with a plain iron gate, and beyond it a straight drive that ran directly to the house across a broad expanse of turn bathed in moonlight. On either side of this the trees ran backward in shallow curves, and encircled by these the grass shimmered like water in a great basin of dark rock. The house was entirely in darkness. But behind it the tower once more rose clear against the sky, all grey stone and dark ivy, and once more a single light shone at the top of it. The whole scene was irresistibly dramatic; it had the simple effectiveness of a well-contrived stage set.

They had come to a halt without a word being spoken. The shadows around them were soft and ambiguous; very faintly, the moonlight seemed still to swim in them. But the party was secure from observation where it stood, and for a time nobody moved. The curiously theatrical effect didn't diminish on a longer view. It was as if the dark curtain of the trees had rolled back on some expected piece of *décor* which had been for some time held in reserve, and which now announced with a satisfactory decisiveness the *dénouement* of the play. And like an admonitory tap upon the boards, an owl hooted rapidly three times.

Almost in the same instant Appleby raised a warning hand. Nobody had been going to speak, and now they all held their breath. From the dark line of trees beyond the turf on their right a figure had emerged. It paused in shadow, and then with slow caution took a few steps forward, apparently to get a clearer view of the house and tower.

"Farquharson!" Timothy breathed the name in Appleby's ear. Appleby nodded but made no reply. The figure turned and glided back into the trees. Some seconds later it could be seen again, briefly emerging from them as if to get round an obstacle. There could be no doubt that Farquharson was taking a covert and circuitous route towards the buildings in front of them.

What seemed to be a long time passed. Appleby's hand remained raised—like that of an umpire, Timothy thought, who indicates to a bowler that he mustn't yet begin play. The owl hooted again, and this time was answered from a distance. Timothy could hear beside him Ian breathing lightly and with care. Probably Ian's shoulder wasn't feeling too good. He must be prevented from trying to climb that tower, if by any chance climbing it was part of whatever enigmatic program lay before them.

Minutes passed in silence. And then, in a low voice, Appleby spoke. "Things aren't going according to plan," he said. "I mean, according to their plan. The timetable's all wrong. David's late. Still, he may be welcomed all the same. We'll let him carry on."

"Just what am I to do?" David did not more than cautiously whisper the words.

"Precisely what I say. Carry on. Forget that you ran out of petrol. Forget that we caught up with you. You're alone. You're fagged out and your judgment's all hay-wire. Your head's full of romantic nonsense—"

"Oh, I say—!"

"Your head's full of romantic nonsense about a girl. And suddenly, just short of Farthing Bishop, you come upon this set-up: the deserted mansion, the ancient tower, the single light. Well, carry on. Do exactly as you'd do if we weren't here. But do it under one limiting condition. You're not to leave ground-level until you hear my voice again.

195

No other voice is to take you a step up that tower, for instance. Do you understand? *No other voice.*"

"I understand."

"Then off you go."

8 THEY WATCHED DAVID walk up to the low iron gate that opened on the drive. For some seconds he stood with his hand on the top bar, gazing at the house. He turned away, retreated, paused, and went back. He climbed the gate. And then in full moonlight he walked directly towards the house.

"Come along." Appleby spoke softly, and vanished into shadow. They followed him for a few yards down a dry ditch. He scrambled through a fence and into the plantation which ran along the road. "We keep among the trees," he said, "and make as little noise as we can, particularly when we get near the tower. Don't, any of you, do anything rash if our friends put on a turn. It will be for David's benefit, not ours."

They continued through the fringe of the trees. David was clearly visible, walking doggedly down the straight drive that led to the house. Once he stopped in his tracks and raised his head, as if glancing up at the solitary light. There was no sign of Farquharson, who had last been glimpsed among the trees dead opposite. The owls had fallen silent and the night was quite still, except for the sound of their own cautious progress towards the tower, and the faint drone of an aeroplane engine very far away.

197

Then suddenly they heard a voice crying out—once, twice —from what seemed a distance almost equally remote or high. It was a woman's voice—and unmistakably calling for help. David had frozen at the first sound. And now he was running headlong towards the tower.

"This is where we hurry too—but still under cover." Appleby had broken into a run, dodging between tree and tree.

Pettifor, who was displaying surprising agility, was the next after him. "You haven't been rash?" he asked urgently. "The boy's all right?"

"Provided he obeys orders he'll be all right." Appleby murmured this over his shoulder. "Or as right as we are. From this point I'd say we share and share alike." For some moments he hurried on, and then stopped and pointed. "There's the doorway. It's open. When we break cover we dash for the wall, hug it close, and then dodge in. David's in already. Come along."

Within seconds they had made their run for the tower and plunged through the doorway into darkness. Then they stood quite still, intent on controlling their breathing. A beam of light shot out. Appleby had produced a torch. They were in a square vaulted chamber with a flagged floor. It was quite bare. And David stood in the centre of it.

Appleby stepped forward, handed him the torch, and without a word pointed to a corner. It held the entrance to a spiral staircase. Appleby moved into the light, beckoned Timothy, and then from his pockets produced two small revolvers. The action was so matter-of-fact that they might have been a pipe and a tobacco pouch. He handed one to Timothy. "Not Service," he whispered. "But there's the safety-catch. Simple as A.B.C." Then he turned to David. "Your show."

198

They crossed to the staircase. David and the torch vanished. In the rapidly fading light Appleby's lips could be seen moving. He might have been counting ten. He nodded and vanished too. Timothy followed, and then Pettifor. They were all climbing. Ian set his teeth and felt for the shaft of the staircase. Some sort of rail or rope would have been a good idea. But he could manage it as it was. He didn't mean to be left down below.

The climb seemed quite as interminable as Ian had expected. At first it was in almost complete darkness, for only the faintest gleam of reflected light from David's torch was visible. Then they came to an ascending series of lancet windows in the wall. They were obscured by the ivy, but dim moonlight filtered through. They passed two dark doorways: they must be to the first and second storeys of the ancient place. Although they were all moving slowly, Ian found that he was dropping behind. If he had tried to cram on speed he would have yelped. And presumably that wouldn't do. Still, he would be in at the death—or whatever fate was going to provide for their being in at. And then, with dramatic suddenness, the show was on. Voices sounded sharply from above. Ian took two steps at a time. And instead of yelping he managed simply to curse. A little extra row didn't matter now.

But when he got to the top there was silence again. He tumbled straight into it. Silence and immobility. It was like a still outside a cinema. And it was gangster stuff that was showing.

This room at the top of the tower was as square and bare as the one at the bottom. It had small windows set in deep embrasures, and in one of these an oil lamp was burning. Part of the roof had vanished, and the greater part, too, of one of the walls. It was this missing wall that gave the final touch, Ian thought, to the theatrical

199

character of the scene: when one turned that way one was facing a dim emptiness faintly powdered with stars, like a vast auditorium during some gala performance with tier upon tier of jewellery reflecting back the light pouring from the stage.

And the full cast—the full cast of those whom the action had not already seen despatched—was assembled in a sort of tableau. They might have been holding desperately to a pose during some hitch in the ringing down of the curtain. Only there was no curtain. And this wasn't a play. It was an actual if bizarre crisis in quite a number of lives.

Dr. Faircloth and Colonel Farquharson faced each other across the empty room. They had the appearance of having been standing thus, poised and wary, before the irruption led by David had taken place. Midway between them, but back by the window where the lamp burned, stood a girl. No doubt this was Alice, whose appearance and character had for a time occupied the exuberant fancies of Pettifor's lot. She didn't, somehow, look much like Faircloth's daughter. She looked less like anybody's daughter than like the orthodox bad woman of the show. But no doubt—Ian rapidly reflected—even the daughters of affluent retired clergymen can stray. And if David had at all fallen for her that morning he must have been in a disturbed state of mind. As for Timothy, he was putting up a very tolerably professional show with his revolver. So was Appleby. But then Appleby, Ian supposed, attended functions of this sort quite in the regular way.

It was Appleby who first spoke. "It seems that this particular devil's broth won't brew," he said. "Too many cooks."

"Perhaps you mean crooks?" It was Farquharson who asked this. He didn't speak with much cordiality. "You seem to be rather fond of thinking them up."

"Criminality in various degree is involved, I think." Appleby looked gravely from Farquharson to Faircloth, and then to the girl. "And now, as we are all present—or all, with one insignificant exception—it will be reasonable to begin."

Faircloth, who had been standing quite still with the air of a man who is thinking hard, vigorously nodded his head. "I quite agree. And it must plainly be your first business, Sir John, to arrest the man Farquharson."

Appleby appeared to consider. "You would advise that?" he asked mildly.

"But most certainly!" Faircloth looked astonished. "Isn't he the blackmailer at the bottom of all this, and have I not just tracked him down to this tower, where I have found him detaining this lady against her will?"

"This lady?" Appleby glanced at the girl again. "Your daughter, I understand?"

"Certainly—my daughter." Faircloth produced this after what might have been a flicker of hesitation. "You know how I was rather anxious at Alice's not having turned up. Then I had a reassuring telegram. Henchman saw it. Judge of my consternation when, later in the evening, I noticed that it had not been despatched from the place where Alice was staying, but from the village of Farthing Bishop! When I recalled all the violent events of the day, my alarm grew. I drove over to investigate, and was attracted by the light in this tower. I climbed up, and discovered my daughter locked in this very room. Then Farquharson arrived, and I had scarcely confronted him when you yourself made your timely appearance. My daughter will tell you how he had carried her off, being aware that, while driving over the moor this morning—"

"Must we really listen to this?" Taking a step forward, Farquharson interrupted angrily. "Don't you perfectly well

201

know—"

"I could do with knowing a good deal more." Appleby's mildness of manner continued. "We've heard Faircloth's explanation of his being here—or least we've heard him beginning to embark on it. Presently, it seems, this rather silent lady is going to take up the tale. But first, Colonel, we might perhaps have a word from you? Perhaps you would care to give your own explanation of your presence?"

"Very well. I got a telephone-call from Faircloth less than an hour ago, saying that he had found his daughter here in this tower, and in distressing circumstances. He begged me to treat his appeal as entirely confidential, and to come over at once. As you can see, I did so."

"Without telling anybody?"

"Certainly. You yourself, Sir John, were not available. But I came—as I think you can guess—in a somewhat more wary manner than Faircloth reckoned on. That is obvious, I imagine, from the fact that I am alive now."

"I see." And Appleby turned to the girl. "Perhaps, madam, you have something to contribute?"

For a moment the girl neither spoke nor moved. David Henchman was staring at her round-eyed. Perhaps he was remembering his persuasion that she was an ordinary sort of girl—the kind one usually met. Then he flushed and looked quickly away. Silently the girl had shrugged her shoulders. It was a small, utterly revealing gesture. The girl wasn't that sort of girl after all.

Appleby had paused for a moment. "Well," he said, "If there is no further spontaneous testimony being offered, I suppose I must say one or two things myself. And I'll begin with the documents in the case. They are three in number. One is no doubt in Dr. Faircloth's pocket: it's his telegram. The second is in my pocket, and is best described as a significant fragment. The third is in Mr. Pettifor's pocket. It's a letter, I think, from his late brother. And it represents the start of the whole series."

"Series?" Pettifor took up the word dully.

"The whole series of murders and attempted murders that have occupied a number of us since round about noon to-day."

9 SLOWLY PETTIFOR HAD brought out his wallet, selected a paper, and handed it to Appleby. "Perhaps," he said quietly, "it needn't be read now. But I'll tell you about it. Soon there will be nobody, I suppose, who reads a newspaper who won't know the whole story of these unlucky deeds. What I was after, of course, was preventing that."

Appleby nodded. "Quite so."

"This letter was sent across by Arthur from Tremlett yesterday morning. It must seem very strange to anybody who didn't know the man. It was to ask me to be on the Loaf, and watching Knack Tor, at noon to-day. I was to wait for an hour, and I was too look not for people, but for a signal. If there was no signal, I was to go away. If there was a signal, I was to go across to the Tor, for Arthur would be needing my support badly. If I saw anybody other than Arthur, I was not to approach them.

"All this was very strange—but my brother went on to hint an explanation. It concerned somebody called Redwine, of whom I had never heard. Redwine was making a demand on him. It was if he had strength to resist that demand that there would be a signal. If there was no signal, he would have given in—and this meant, he added, that he would be done for, although it was possible that nobody would ever know."

Pettifor paused. And Faircloth looked across at Farquharson. "Blackmail," he said decisively.

"Yes—blackmail." It was Pettifor who replied. "I could see no other explanation. As I have explained to Sir John, my brother was deeply sensitive about certain events in his earlier life, and there were some that he would have died rather than have made known. Even so, and even although my brother's character was such that his strange letter was now wholly inexplicable to me, there was something in it that puzzled me. It was, I think, the sense it conveyed of some unknown degradation facing him, and of some moral issue that he must confront utterly alone. At least I knew him well enough to see that there was nothing I could do except carry out his instructions. I did so. Or I tried to do so. But unfortunately I failed."

David interrupted. "You mean, sir, you were on the Loaf?"

"No. I took the road to the north of the moor—not that by which you yourself approached Knack Tor—and during the run my car broke down. It took me, being a poor mechanic, more than half an hour to put it right. When I began my walk across the moor, I was still much behind my time. And then I saw what could only be Arthur's signal. It was a thin column of smoke going up from the summit of the Tor. I felt an immense sense of relief. Obscure as the whole matter was, I recalled that Arthur never misused words. If he had declared that a signal would mean that he had found strength to resist something wrong, then it was so. But if he had declared that he would then sorely need my support, that was so also. I hurried on. The smoke faded and vanished when I had still nearly a mile of heavy going before me. When I reached the summit, it was to find my brother dead. He had been shot through the forehead. But there was no weapon to be seen.

"Strange as it must seem, I acted before I allowed myself to feel. I hurried, that is to say, to the farther verge of the summit, and scanned the moor. I was just in time to see two figures vanish along the track."

"In fact, sir, you saw Redwine and his assistant going after me." David said this hesitantly. He didn't much like to interrupt.

"No doubt. Well, then I did feel. I was overcome with grief and horror and bewilderment. I sat by my brother's dead body for a very long time."

Appleby, who had been standing quite immobile during this narrative, stirred slightly and asked a question. "Really a very long time? Sometimes one can feel that quite a short interval is that."

"Certainly for more than an hour. Slowly, during that interval, my mind became capable of intellectual operation. Uncertainly at first, and then with full conviction, there came to me a sense of what lay at the bottom of the tragedy. Arthur's signal, I saw, had been something more than a signal. It had itself been an honourable deed. And he had paid for it with his life. Yet in the world's opinion his death would be a disgraceful one. I saw that I had a duty—to my brother and to our name. But a duty can be one thing, and any practical means towards fulfilling it may be quite another. I was brooding on my problems—for I had, thank God, seen that I had a problem—when I was startled by voices at the base of the rock. They were the voices of two men."

"Sir John and me!" David blurted this out.

"No, no. This was hours before that." Pettifor smiled faintly. "I doubt whether you had yet possessed yourself of Ian's famous horse."

"Did you recognize either voice?" Appleby asked.

"No. It would not, in my alarm, have been easy to do so. And perhaps my immediate action was unaccountable. But I felt instantly that here was danger—and danger which I could do no good by facing. I ran to the farther side of the summit, descended with what speed my small skill permitted, and concealed myself as best I could at the bottom. Virtually simultaneously, the new arrivals were scaling the other side, and presently—although very faintly—I could hear them talking again above. I realised that they were quarrelling. And then there was a shot . . . and silence."

Pettifor had paused, and for a moment nobody said a word. Then Faircloth once again gave his decisive nod. It was as if he felt a clear picture to be building itself up in his mind. "In fact," he said, "thieves—or blackmailers— were falling out."

Pettifor nodded, but not as if he had much attended to the words. "I remained hidden," he said, "for ten minutes or more. There continued to be no sound from above, and at length I resolved to climb back to the summit. What I found there, you can guess. There was now another dead man. I was so staggered that for some minutes I could do nothing to the purpose. Then I crossed to the farther verge. A single figure was retreating from the Tor—much where I had seen the two figures running rather more than an hour before. But this figure was merely walking rapidly away."

Appleby glanced from Faircloth to Farquharson. "But you couldn't identify it?"

Pettifor shook his head. "My sight is no longer very good at distances. And now I come to that part of my narrative which I would most willingly spare myself the recital of.

I would beg you to remember that my moral position was a very difficult one. It is possible that what I did cannot be justified by any moral considerations—as it certainly cannot be in law."

"My dear sir"—Faircloth spoke with easy benevolence—"you may be assured of our sympathy in anything you have to relate."

"Thank you." For a moment Pettifor appeared bewildered, and then he went on. "The two bodies—my brother's and the stranger's—lay, or had been disposed, in a manner suggesting a gun-fight or duel—with a pistol in, or near, the hand of each. The third man, that is to say, had killed his companion, and left this appearance of an affray between that companion and my brother. I saw no comfort in this contrivance. And suddenly my resolution was taken. I must get my brother's body away. I had already known, indeed, that my duty lay there. And now, under the stress of this new and fantastic situation, a bold plan came to me. I too could contrive the appearance of something. If Arthur's body was found in its present situation—indeed, if it was ever found at all—nothing could prevent scandalous revelation and speculation. Therefore it must vanish. And I very well knew where, not half a mile away, it could vanish—and for ever. I remembered too that my car, although unpretentious, could be got over the moor. It had been given me by Arthur, who had used it on his own land. It would not be indecent, I concluded, to employ it as his hearse. So I set off to see if I could, in fact, bring it up to the Tor. The task proved surprisingly easy. I climbed again to the summit. I removed the small pistol which had been set in Redwine's hand, and substituted for it that which had been set in my brother's—and from which had come, of course, the shot with which Redwine had been killed. What I should leave on the summit, therefore, was simply the appearance of a suicide. It was utterly unknown to me, remember, that David had been on the summit and actually seen—perhaps even recognised—my brother's body."

"I certainly didn't recognise him," David said. "I'd never met him. But he did seem vaguely familiar. I suppose it was a family likeness."

"My plan, so hazardous in the conception, was turning out to be surprisingly simple in execution. There was one very bad moment, which I can hardly bring myself to mention. I had no means of lowering Arthur's body to the ground. I had to enforce upon myself, therefore, the clear distinction between what was merely mortal in his remains and what of a higher and immaterial nature I was concerned to preserve: his reputation after death. I threw the body down."

"And then—according to your view of the matter—all went well?" Appleby asked this a shade hastily.

"Certainly. There was a little difficulty later in getting the body far enough into the bog I had chosen. But I managed it. Arthur was of a spare physique."

"I see. That, of course, was fortunate."

Pettifor nodded—and the vein of fanaticism in him appeared oddly in the gesture. "I had, of course, stripped the body. It was thus that I was able to motor immediately to Tremlett and contrive the appearance of the drowning accident. When I returned to Nymph Monachorum, and found Faircloth proposing a visit to Knack Tor, I was naturally rather startled at first. But on second thoughts the proposal commended itself to me. I should be present at the discovery of Redwine's body, and be a witness to the marked appearance of suicide. But the affair of the man in knickerbockers, and the revelation of David's adventures, showed me that all was not to be plain sailing

209

after all. And the situation, as you know, was soon entirely out of my control."

"Fortunately it isn't out of the control of the police." Faircloth contrived to say this not at all like a man who is being steadily covered by a revolver. "May we now hear something about what has been called the third exhibit?"

Appleby turned to him. "Most certainly. The third exhibit was discovered by me in the fireplace of the late Mr. Arthur Pettifor's study at Tremlett. It is a typescript communication, partly consumed by fire. But there is no obscurity about its meaning. It is an attempt to extort a large sum of money from Arthur Pettifor by menaces. And it makes an appointment on Knack Tor."

"Most interesting—most significant." Faircloth paused. "And is there any means of telling where this blackmailing letter came from?"

Appleby nodded. "Certainly there is. It was typed on Colonel Farquharson's machine, which is now in his room at the George. I think it's not too much to say that we have a clear case." And Appleby turned to Farquharson. "You agree?"

Farquharson considered this impassively for a moment. "Yes," he said, "I certainly agree. But there's a little more to mention, is there not?"

"There is." The revolver was very steady in Appleby's hand. "The typescript fragments purports, of course, to have been written yesterday, at the latest. But—as I have explained to the Colonel—it was in fact produced on the machine late this evening."

"Fantastic!" Faircloth's voice rose in a sudden shout.

"Not at all. The type-face bears the trace of a small but unmistakable mutilation which I effected myself, with my penknife and in the presence of two witnesses, scarcely a couple of hours ago."

210

There was a moment's dead silence. It was broken not by a voice, but by a sudden shattering of glass. With a single swift movement the hitherto immobile girl had hurled the oil lamp to the floor.

What followed, followed in a flash. Open to the night though it was, the room seemed for a moment quite dark. Appleby sprang to bar the way to the staircase. Timothy made for Faircloth and bumped into David, who switched on the torch. The girl was standing where she had stood before. Pettifor had hurried to the gap in the farther wall, and was peering queerly out and down. Faircloth had vanished.

"He hasn't jumped?" Appleby shouted this from the door.

"No, no—the ivy . . . he's trying to climb down." Pettifor was leaning far out. "Stop, man!" he called. "It's tearing . . . keep still . . . Faircloth, quick . . . my arm . . . grab, man . . . *grab!*" He leant out further. There was a rending sound, a despairing cry from Faircloth, and then silence. Pettifor had gone. Where he had been a moment before there was only dust, drifting up and in from the ivy, dancing in the cold pale light from the moon.

10 APPLEBY WAS AT the George not long after breakfast next day. He found David Henchman sitting wanly in an obscure corner of the garden. He sat down beside him. "Ian Dancer not too bad?" he asked.

"Not too bad. He's had to have a doctor again. But he's up." David poked idly at the ground with his toe. "Ogg's taken it very well."

Appleby nodded. "Ogg's all right." It pleased him to remember that this had been Pettifor's opinion too.

"Shaved off that beard. Says he must do the fair thing by the tenants, and get their confidence. They might distrust a beard in so young a squire."

"Good lord!" Appleby felt suddenly rather old. It was a feeling one got sometimes, when confronted with the incredible resilience of the young.

There was a long pause. "Did he know?" David asked.

"Did Pettifor know about Faircloth—that he was the man ultimately responsible for his brother's death? Yes, he'd tumbled to it, all right. But it didn't make any odds, when it came to stretching out an arm to a falling man."

"No." David considered. "Rather a good show," he said.

"Eh? Oh, yes—decidedly." Appleby looked at David curiously. The boy seemed quite unaware of any echo in his words. "Well," he went on, "at least it's all cleared up. That's what I came out to tell you . . . to tell all of Pettifor's lot. The girl talked."

"Oh—the girl." David said this very coldly.

"And we've got last night's insignificant absentee—the First Assistant, or whatever we called him. But he doesn't know much."

"It really was spy stuff?"

"Decidedly. What Faircloth and Redwine were after wasn't, of course, money. That cropped up only in the typewritten scrap faked and planted by Faircloth, after I'd told him a whopping lie about Farquharson being a notorious blackmailer. It was a crude trap. But Faircloth fell right in."

"It wasn't money? It was secrets?"

"Yes. Arthur Pettifor, as a high-up man with a scientific background, had access to a lot. I got on to that quickly enough. What he was told to bring to the Tor was . . . well, you can call it a document of state. And they planned to get lots more out of him, too. But he rallied. He sent that document up in smoke pretty well under Redwine's nose—and then told him to publish and be damned. Redwine instantly saw that he was ruined. If Arthur Pettifor defied him and went to the police, Redwine's whole game would be uncovered and he'd go to gaol. So he shot Pettifor out of hand. Then, together with First Assistant, he went after you. But Faircloth, who was the real boss, and who was lurking around—he'd been brought, you know, by the girl he passed off as his daughter—Faircloth pulled Redwine out of the chase, leaving it to First Assistant and the man in knickerbockers. Faircloth felt in no danger, for you hadn't spotted him. He took Redwine back to the Tor, I imagine, because he didn't trust his story. And quite soon his distrust mounted to a point at which he decided poor Redwine would be better liquidated. So he shot him there and then, arranged the appearance of that obscure affray, and made off. He hadn't much else to fear. But he knew you mustn't get another sight of the girl. That really meant that you must be liquidated too. Hence his spurious telegram, which he trusted to your spotting was spurious, and the subsequent trap he improvised for your romantic temperament. At the same time he sent his appeal for help to Farquharson—whom he still believed to be, by the greatest good fortune in the world, a blackmailer notorious to the police. It was you who were to fall from the top of that tower—and Farquharson, too. But I'd told Farquharson quite a lot. And you, by the grace of God, ran out of petrol. So the scheme failed. In a way, it deserved to."

"Deserved to?"

"It was a crack-pot scheme. But a brilliant improvisation, all the same."

"What made you lay that trap with Farquharson's typewriter? How had Faircloth given himself away?"

"By very carelessly saying something about the affair being a matter of national security, or something of the sort. I'd said not a word about that, and he oughtn't to have known."

David reflected. "And that's all?"

"That's all."

David stretched himself as he sat. The mild sunshine was beginning to bring a faint, luxurious warmth to the garden. "I say," he asked, "could you do a walk with me this afternoon—to Knack Tor? I've remembered something. I left my walking stick. Rather a nice stick, you said."

Appleby got up. "Yes," he said. "Straight after lunch." And as he walked away he murmured to himself again: "Good lord!"

214

THE PERENNIAL LIBRARY MYSTERY SERIES

Delano Ames

CORPSE DIPLOMATIQUE   P 637, $2.84
"Sprightly and intelligent."

—New York Herald Tribune Book Review

FOR OLD CRIME'S SAKE   P 629, $2.84

MURDER, MAESTRO, PLEASE   P 630, $2.84
"If there is a more engaging couple in modern fiction than Jane and
Dagobert Brown, we have not met them."   *—Scotsman*

SHE SHALL HAVE MURDER   P 638, $2.84
"Combines the merit of both the English and American schools in the
new mystery. It's as breezy as the best of the American ones, and has
the sophistication and wit of any top-notch Britisher."

—New York Herald Tribune Book Review

E. C. Bentley

TRENT'S LAST CASE   P 440, $2.50
"One of the three best detective stories ever written."

—Agatha Christie

TRENT'S OWN CASE   P 516, $2.25
"I won't waste time saying that the plot is sound and the detection
satisfying. Trent has not altered a scrap and reappears with all his old
humor and charm."   *—Dorothy L. Sayers*

Gavin Black

A DRAGON FOR CHRISTMAS   P 473, $1.95
"Potent excitement!"   *—New York Herald Tribune*

THE EYES AROUND ME   P 485, $1.95
"I stayed up until all hours last night reading *The Eyes Around Me,*
which is something I do not do very often, but I was so intrigued by the
ingeniousness of Mr. Black's plotting and the witty way in which he spins
his mystery. I can only say that I enjoyed the book enormously."

—F. van Wyck Mason

YOU WANT TO DIE, JOHNNY?   P 472, $1.95
"Gavin Black doesn't just develop a pressure plot in suspense, he adds
uninfected wit, character, charm, and sharp knowledge of the Far East
to make rereading as keen as the first race-through."   *—Book Week*

Nicholas Blake (cont'd)

THOU SHELL OF DEATH   P 428, $1.95

"It has all the virtues of culture, intelligence and sensibility that the most exacting connoisseur could ask of detective fiction."

— *The Times* [London] *Literary Supplement*

THE WIDOW'S CRUISE   P 399, $2.25

"A stirring suspense. . . . The thrilling tale leaves nothing to be desired."

— *Springfield Republican*

THE WORM OF DEATH   P 400, $2.25

"It [The Worm of Death] is one of Blake's very best—and his best is better than almost anyone's."   — Louis Untermeyer

John & Emery Bonett

A BANNER FOR PEGASUS   P 554, $2.40

"A gem! Beautifully plotted and set. . . . Not only is the murder adroit and deserved, and the detection competent, but the love story is charming."   — Jacques Barzun and Wendell Hertig Taylor

DEAD LION   P 563, $2.40

"A clever plot, authentic background and interesting characters highly recommended this one."   — *New Republic*

Christianna Brand

GREEN FOR DANGER   P 551, $2.50

"You have to reach for the greatest of Great Names (Christie, Carr, Queen . . .) to find Brand's rivals in the devious subtleties of the trade."

— Anthony Boucher

TOUR DE FORCE   P 572, $2.40

"Complete with traps for the over-ingenious, a double-reverse surprise ending and a key clue planted so fairly and obviously that you completely overlook it. If that's your idea of perfect entertainment, then seize at once upon *Tour de Force.*"   — Anthony Boucher, *The New York Times*

James Byrom

OR BE HE DEAD   P 585, $2.84

"A very original tale . . . Well written and steadily entertaining."

— Jacques Barzun & Wendell Hertig Taylor, *A Catalogue of Crime*

Henry Calvin

IT'S DIFFERENT ABROAD   P 640, $2.84
"What is remarkable and delightful, Mr. Calvin imparts a flavor of satire to what he renovates and compels us to take straight."

—Jacques Barzun

Marjorie Carleton

VANISHED   P 559, $2.40
"Exceptional . . . a minor triumph."
—Jacques Barzun and Wendell Hertig Taylor, *A Catalogue of Crime*

George Harmon Coxe

MURDER WITH PICTURES   P 527, $2.25
"[Coxe] has hit the bull's-eye with his first shot."

—*The New York Times*

Edmund Crispin

BURIED FOR PLEASURE   P 506, $2.50
"Absolute and unalloyed delight."

—Anthony Boucher, *The New York Times*

Lionel Davidson

THE MENORAH MEN   P 592, $2.84
"Of his fellow thriller writers, only John Le Carré shows the same instinct for the viscera."   —*Chicago Tribune*

NIGHT OF WENCESLAS   P 595, $2.84
"A most ingenious thriller, so enriched with style, wit, and a sense of serious comedy that it all but transcends its kind."

—*The New Yorker*

THE ROSE OF TIBET   P 593, $2.84
"I hadn't realized how much I missed the genuine Adventure story . . . until I read *The Rose of Tibet*."   —Graham Greene

D. M. Devine

MY BROTHER'S KILLER   P 558, $2.40
"A most enjoyable crime story which I enjoyed reading down to the last moment."   —Agatha Christie

Kenneth Fearing

THE BIG CLOCK   P 500, $1.95
"It will be some time before chill-hungry clients meet again so rare a compound of irony, satire, and icy-fingered narrative. *The Big Clock* is . . . a psychothriller you won't put down." —*Weekly Book Review*

Andrew Garve

THE ASHES OF LODA   P 430, $1.50
"Garve . . . embellishes a fine fast adventure story with a more credible picture of the U.S.S.R. than is offered in most thrillers."
—*The New York Times Book Review*

THE CUCKOO LINE AFFAIR   P 451, $1.95
". . . an agreeable and ingenious piece of work." —*The New Yorker*

A HERO FOR LEANDA   P 429, $1.50
"One can trust Mr. Garve to put a fresh twist to any situation, and the ending is really a lovely surprise." —*The Manchester Guardian*

MURDER THROUGH THE LOOKING GLASS   P 449, $1.95
". . . refreshingly out-of-the-way and enjoyable . . . highly recommended to all comers." —*Saturday Review*

NO TEARS FOR HILDA   P 441, $1.95
"It starts fine and finishes finer. I got behind on breathing watching Max get not only his man but his woman, too." —Rex Stout

THE RIDDLE OF SAMSON   P 450, $1.95
"The story is an excellent one, the people are quite likable, and the writing is superior." —*Springfield Republican*

Michael Gilbert

BLOOD AND JUDGMENT   P 446, $1.95
"Gilbert readers need scarcely be told that the characters all come alive at first sight, and that his surpassing talent for narration enhances any plot. . . . Don't miss." —*San Francisco Chronicle*

THE BODY OF A GIRL   P 459, $1.95
"Does what a good mystery should do: open up into all kinds of ramifications, with untold menace behind the action. At the end, there is a bang-up climax, and it is a pleasure to see how skilfully Gilbert wraps everything up." —*The New York Times Book Review*

Michael Gilbert (cont'd)

THE DANGER WITHIN   P 448, $1.95

"Michael Gilbert has nicely combined some elements of the straight detective story with plenty of action, suspense, and adventure, to produce a superior thriller."   —*Saturday Review*

FEAR TO TREAD   P 458, $1.95

"Merits serious consideration as a work of art."

—*The New York Times*

Joe Gores

HAMMETT   P 631, $2.84

"Joe Gores at his very best. Terse, powerful writing—with the master, Dashiell Hammett, as the protagonist in a novel I think he would have been proud to call his own."   —Robert Ludlum

C. W. Grafton

BEYOND A REASONABLE DOUBT   P 519, $1.95

"A very ingenious tale of murder . . . a brilliant and gripping narrative."
—Jacques Barzun and Wendell Hertig Taylor

THE RAT BEGAN TO GNAW THE ROPE   P 639, $2.84

"Fast, humorous story with flashes of brilliance."

—*The New Yorker*

Edward Grierson

THE SECOND MAN   P 528, $2.25

"One of the best trial-testimony books to have come along in quite a while."   —*The New Yorker*

Bruce Hamilton

TOO MUCH OF WATER   P 635, $2.84

"A superb sea mystery. . . . The prose is excellent."
—Jacques Barzun and Wendell Hertig Taylor, *A Catalogue of Crime*

Cyril Hare

DEATH IS NO SPORTSMAN   P 555, $2.40

"You will be thrilled because it succeeds in placing an ingenious story in a new and refreshing setting. . . . The identity of the murderer is really a surprise."   —*Daily Mirror*

DEATH WALKS THE WOODS   P 556, $2.40

"Here is a fine formal detective story, with a technically brilliant solution demanding the attention of all connoisseurs of construction."

—Anthony Boucher, *The New York Times Book Review*

AN ENGLISH MURDER   P 455, $2.50

"By a long shot, the best crime story I have read for a long time. Everything is traditional, but originality does not suffer. The setting is perfect. Full marks to Mr. Hare."   —*Irish Press*

SUICIDE EXCEPTED   P 636, $2.84

"Adroit in its manipulation . . . and distinguished by a plot-twister which I'll wager Christie wishes she'd thought of."

—*The New York Times*

TENANT FOR DEATH   P 570, $2.84

"The way in which an air of probability is combined both with clear, terse narrative and with a good deal of subtle suburban atmosphere, proves the extreme skill of the writer."   —*The Spectator*

TRAGEDY AT LAW   P 522, $2.25

"An extremely urbane and well-written detective story."

—*The New York Times*

UNTIMELY DEATH   P 514, $2.25

"The English detective story at its quiet best, meticulously underplayed, rich in perceivings of the droll human animal and ready at the last with a neat surprise which has been there all the while had we but wits to see it."   —*New York Herald Tribune Book Review*

THE WIND BLOWS DEATH   P 589, $2.84

"A plot compounded of musical knowledge, a Dickens allusion, and a subtle point in law is related with delightfully unobtrusive wit, warmth, and style."   —*The New York Times*

WITH A BARE BODKIN   P 523, $2.25

"One of the best detective stories published for a long time."

—*The Spectator*

Robert Harling

THE ENORMOUS SHADOW   P 545, $2.50

"In some ways the best spy story of the modern period. . . . The writing is terse and vivid . . . the ending full of action . . . altogether first-rate."

—Jacques Barzun and Wendell Hertig Taylor, *A Catalogue of Crime*

Matthew Head

THE CABINDA AFFAIR P 541, $2.25
"An absorbing whodunit and a distinguished novel of atmosphere."
—Anthony Boucher, *The New York Times*

THE CONGO VENUS P 597, $2.84
"Terrific. The dialogue is just plain wonderful."
—*The Boston Globe*

MURDER AT THE FLEA CLUB P 542, $2.50
"The true delight is in Head's style, its limpid ease combined with humor and an awesome precision of phrase." —*San Francisco Chronicle*

M. V. Heberden

ENGAGED TO MURDER P 533, $2.25
"Smooth plotting." —*The New York Times*

James Hilton

WAS IT MURDER? P 501, $1.95
"The story is well planned and well written."
—*The New York Times*

P. M. Hubbard

HIGH TIDE P 571, $2.40
"A smooth elaboration of mounting horror and danger."
—*Library Journal*

Elspeth Huxley

THE AFRICAN POISON MURDERS P 540, $2.25
"Obscure venom, manical mutilations, deadly bush fire, thrilling climax compose major opus.... Top-flight."
—*Saturday Review of Literature*

MURDER ON SAFARI P 587, $2.84
"Right now we'd call Mrs. Huxley a dangerous rival to Agatha Christie." —*Books*

Francis Iles

BEFORE THE FACT   P 517, $2.50

"Not many 'serious' novelists have produced character studies to compare with Iles's internally terrifying portrait of the murderer in *Before the Fact*, his masterpiece and a work truly deserving the appellation of unique and beyond price."

—Howard Haycraft

MALICE AFORETHOUGHT   P 532, $1.95

"It is a long time since I have read anything so good as *Malice Aforethought*, with its cynical humour, acute criminology, plausible detail and rapid movement. It makes you hug yourself with pleasure."

—H. C. Harwood, *Saturday Review*

Michael Innes

THE CASE OF THE JOURNEYING BOY   P 632, $3.12

"I could see no faults in it. There is no one to compare with him."

—*Illustrated London News*

DEATH BY WATER   P 574, $2.40

"The amount of ironic social criticism and deft characterization of scenes and people would serve another author for six books."

—Jacques Barzun and Wendell Hertig Taylor

HARE SITTING UP   P 590, $2.84

"There is hardly anyone (in mysteries or mainstream) more exquisitely literate, allusive and Jamesian—and hardly anyone with a firmer sense of melodramatic plot or a more vigorous gift of storytelling."

—Anthony Boucher, *The New York Times*

THE LONG FAREWELL   P 575, $2.40

"A model of the deft, classic detective story, told in the most wittily diverting prose."   —*The New York Times*

THE MAN FROM THE SEA   P 591, $2.84

"The pace is brisk, the adventures exciting and excitingly told, and above all he keeps to the very end the interesting ambiguity of the man from the sea."

—*New Statesman*

THE SECRET VANGUARD   P 584, $2.84

"Innes . . . has mastered the art of swift, exciting and well-organized narrative."   —*The New York Times*

THE WEIGHT OF THE EVIDENCE   P 633, $2.84

"First-class puzzle, deftly solved. University background interesting and amusing."   —*Saturday Review of Literature*

Mary Kelly

THE SPOILT KILL P 565, $2.40
"Mary Kelly is a new Dorothy Sayers. . . . [An] exciting new novel."
—*Evening News*

Lange Lewis

THE BIRTHDAY MURDER P 518, $1.95
"Almost perfect in its playlike purity and delightful prose."
—Jacques Barzun and Wendell Hertig Taylor

Allan MacKinnon

HOUSE OF DARKNESS P 582, $2.84
"His best . . . a perfect compendium."
—Jacques Barzun & Wendell Hertig Taylor, *A Catalogue of Crime*

Arthur Maling

LUCKY DEVIL P 482, $1.95
"The plot unravels at a fast clip, the writing is breezy and Maling's approach is as fresh as today's stockmarket quotes."
—*Louisville Courier Journal*

RIPOFF P 483, $1.95
"A swiftly paced story of today's big business is larded with intrigue as a Ralph Nader-type investigates an insurance scandal and is soon on the run from a hired gun and his brother. . . . Engrossing and credible."
—*Booklist*

SCHROEDER'S GAME P 484, $1.95
"As the title indicates, this Schroeder is up to something, and the unravelling of his game is a diverting and sufficiently blood-soaked entertainment."
—*The New Yorker*

Austin Ripley

MINUTE MYSTERIES P 387, $2.50
More than one hundred of the world's shortest detective stories. Only one possible solution to each case!

Thomas Sterling

THE EVIL OF THE DAY P 529, $2.50
"Prose as witty and subtle as it is sharp and clear. . .characters unconventionally conceived and richly bodied forth . . . . In short, a novel to be treasured."
—Anthony Boucher, *The New York Times*

Julian Symons

THE BELTING INHERITANCE P 468, $1.95
"A superb whodunit in the best tradition of the detective story."
— August Derleth, *Madison Capital Times*

BLAND BEGINNING P 469, $1.95
"Mr. Symons displays a deft storytelling skill, a quiet and literate wit, a nice feeling for character, and detectival ingenuity of a high order."
— Anthony Boucher, *The New York Times*

BOGUE'S FORTUNE P 481, $1.95
"There's a touch of the old sardonic humour, and more than a touch of style."
— *The Spectator*

THE BROKEN PENNY P 480, $1.95
"The most exciting, astonishing and believable spy story to appear in years.
— Anthony Boucher, *The New York Times Book Review*

THE COLOR OF MURDER P 461, $1.95
"A singularly unostentatious and memorably brilliant detective story."
— *New York Herald Tribune Book Review*

Dorothy Stockbridge Tillet
(John Stephen Strange)

THE MAN WHO KILLED FORTESCUE P 536, $2.25
"Better than average."
— *Saturday Review of Literature*

Simon Troy

THE ROAD TO RHUINE P 583, $2.84
"Unusual and agreeably told."
— *San Francisco Chronicle*

SWIFT TO ITS CLOSE P 546, $2.40
"A nicely literate British mystery . . . the atmosphere and the plot are exceptionally well wrought, the dialogue excellent."
— *Best Sellers*

Henry Wade

THE DUKE OF YORK'S STEPS P 588, $2.84
"A classic of the golden age."
— Jacques Barzun & Wendell Hertig Taylor, *A Catalogue of Crime*

A DYING FALL P 543, $2.50
"One of those expert British suspense jobs . . . it crackles with undercurrents of blackmail, violent passion and murder. Topnotch in its class."
— *Time*

THE HANGING CAPTAIN　　　　　　　　　　P 548, $2.50
"This is a detective story for connoisseurs, for those who value clear thinking and good writing above mere ingenuity and easy thrills."
　　　　　　　　　　　　　　　—*Times Literary Supplement*

Hillary Waugh

LAST SEEN WEARING . . .　　　　　　　　P 552, $2.40
"A brilliant tour de force."　　　　　　　　—Julian Symons

THE MISSING MAN　　　　　　　　　　　　P 553, $2.40
"The quiet detailed police work of Chief Fred C. Fellows, Stockford, Conn., is at its best in *The Missing Man* . . . one of the Chief's toughest cases and one of the best handled."
　　　　　　—Anthony Boucher, *The New York Times Book Review*

Henry Kitchell Webster

WHO IS THE NEXT?　　　　　　　　　　　P 539, $2.25
"A double murder, private-plane piloting, a neat impersonation, and a delicate courtship are adroitly combined by a writer who knows how to use the language."　　—Jacques Barzun and Wendell Hertig Taylor

Anna Mary Wells

MURDERER'S CHOICE　　　　　　　　　　P 534, $2.50
"Good writing, ample action, and excellent character work."
　　　　　　　　　　　　　—*Saturday Review of Literature*

A TALENT FOR MURDER　　　　　　　　　P 535, $2.25
"The discovery of the villain is a decided shock."　　　—*Books*

Edward Young

THE FIFTH PASSENGER　　　　　　　　　P 544, $2.25
"Clever and adroit . . . excellent thriller . . ."　—*Library Journal*

If you enjoyed this book you'll want to know about
THE PERENNIAL LIBRARY MYSTERY SERIES

Buy them at your local bookstore or use this coupon for ordering:

Qty	P number	Price
	postage and handling charge	$1.00
	_____ book(s) @ $0.25	
	TOTAL	

Prices contained in this coupon are Harper & Row invoice prices only.
They are subject to change without notice, and in no way reflect the prices at which these books may be sold by other suppliers.

HARPER & ROW, Mail Order Dept. #PMS, 10 East 53rd St., New York, N.Y. 10022.
Please send me the books I have checked above. I am enclosing $_____
which includes a postage and handling charge of $1.00 for the first book and 25¢ for each additional book. Send check or money order. No cash or C.O.D.s please

Name_____

Address_____

City_____ State_____ Zip_____
Please allow 4 weeks for delivery. USA only. This offer expires 12/31/84
Please add applicable sales tax.